APR 1 9 2010

FABULOUS

A Pace Academy Novel
The Pacesetters...can you keep up!

CHEROKEE

APR 1 9 2010

Simone Bryant

FABULOUS

KIMANI
tru
™

If you purchased this book without a cover you should be aware that this book is stolen property. It was reported as "unsold and destroyed" to the publisher, and neither the author nor the publisher has received any payment for this "stripped book."

Recycling programs
for this product may
not exist in your area.

FABULOUS

ISBN-13: 978-0-373-83126-5

© 2010 by Niobia Bryant

All rights reserved. The reproduction, transmission or utilization of this work in whole or in part in any form by any electronic, mechanical or other means, now known or hereafter invented, including xerography, photocopying and recording, or in any information storage or retrieval system, is forbidden without written permission. For permission please contact Kimani Press, Editorial Office, 233 Broadway, New York, NY 10279 U.S.A.

This book is a work of fiction. The names, characters, incidents and places are the products of the author's imagination, and are not to be construed as real. While the author was inspired in part by actual events, none of the characters in the book is based on an actual person. Any resemblance to persons living or dead is entirely coincidental and unintentional.

® and TM are trademarks owned and used by the trademark owner and/or its licensee. Trademarks indicated with ® are registered in the United States Patent and Trademark Office, the Canadian Trade Marks Office and/or other countries.

www.KimaniTRU.com

Printed in U.S.A.

For my nephew,
Kal-El

"Auntie loves the baby…"

Acknowledgments

Mama, I love & miss U.

Tony, I adore & need U.

Caleb, I look up 2 & admire U.

Hajah & Kal-El, I cherish & treasure U both.

Khadejah and Krystal,
now THESE books of mine are for U two 2 read. ;-)

Evette, thank U for that skillful red pen.

To the Harlequin, Kimani TRU team thanx 4 everything U all did 2 support & promote this book. UR excitement about it made me want 2 see it in print even more.

Thank U in advance 2 all the readers of this book,
the book clubs that may select it, the libraries that will carry it and all bookstores/street vendors that will sell it.

To all the little girls and young ladies with their eyes on the prize, never be afraid to be 4ever Fabulous in any and everything U do.
Be a pacesetter 24/7.

And last but not least, thank you 2 my Pacesetter clique for nudging me gently to breathe literary life into the three of U.

pacesetters
[payss setters] (n):
a group regarded as being leaders in any field and one whom others may emulate. (i.e.: pacemakers, innovators, pacers, modernizers, leaders, leading lights, pioneers, trendsetters)

fabulous
[fabbyɕlɛss] (adj):
amazingly or almost unbelievably great or impressive; excellent; extremely good, pleasant, or enjoyable

the Beginning

WE were destined from birth to be on top. The best. The cream of the crop. The elite. Age means nothing. The only things that matter are the number of zeroes in our parents' bank accounts and the size of our trust funds.

All eyes are on us at all times whenever we walk through the halls of Pace Academy. They are always watching and copying our style, our moves, everything we do.

We run Pace Academy

We determine who and what is in and out.

We set the pace.

Welcome to *OUR* world.

one

"**Just** a little over a month till my b-day."

Starr Lester replaced the cap on the pink-and-white glitter pen that she'd just used to draw an X on the calendar. October 2. She couldn't *wait* for her birthday. She'd given her parents her wish list weeks ago and expected that they would get everything on it.

With short, neatly trimmed nails painted in her favorite Cinnamon Sugar, Starr fingered the Tiffany diamond pendants she wore on thin gold chains around her neck. One was a star and the other spelled out *Blessed*.

Life as the daughter of Cole Lester, multiplatinum R&B-singer-turned-owner of TopStarr Records, was good—*real* good.

She had her own chauffeur-driven Bentley, free use of her daddy's black American Express card *and* a weekly allowance. She even had her own spacious suite in her parents' sprawling Bernardsville, New Jersey, mansion.

Her wing of the house included a spacious circular bedroom, a spa bathroom with a Jacuzzi tub, a river-rock shower stall and heated floors throughout. There was a screening room with its own fully stocked snack bar, a custom walk-in closet with shelves and organizers that resembled a small clothing boutique, her own private balcony with an outdoor fireplace and security cameras outside her door with an electronic keypad that only she and her parents had the combination to. Mostly, Starr loved, loved, loved that every square foot was designed to suit her tastes.

The suite had started out as a luxurious garden-themed nursery. Later it was decorated with her favorite cartoon characters and bright neon colors. And for her thirteenth birthday, her parents had brought in their decorator and given Starr carte blanche to make it her teen haven.

The entire suite had a classic, beautiful style with French country cream-colored painted furniture and pops of her favorite color—fuchsia. Everything—the linens, the floor-length silk curtains, the plush cream-colored carpet—was luxurious. The cathedral ceiling gave a feeling of spaciousness. She had every creature comfort at her fingertips, including a sixty-inch plasma TV that was mounted over a remote-controlled fireplace. The window seat and club chairs offered a comfy place to lounge with her friends.

And the comforts of being Starr went beyond her living quarters.

She had her own part-time personal assistant, a full-time maid and an on-call personal trainer. Then there were the celebrity godparents and the offspring of the rich and famous, who made up her circle of friends. She had anything and everything her heart desired.

Humph, there was no way Starr could really complain. Well, not most of the time anyway.

Bzzzzz.

Her dark eyes shifted over to the intercom system on the corner of her desk. She rolled her eyes at the interruption. "Yes?" she said aloud, her voice husky and soft even at the young age of fourteen-going-on-fifteen-soon.

"Starr, come on down. Your father's home early and we're going to eat dinner together."

Shocker. Usually her dad was never home this early and most nights she ate dinner in the kitchen with Justine, the cook, or in the comfort and security of her bedroom suite.

"Coming, Mom," Starr replied as she plopped into the fuchsia leather Parsons chair in front of her desk. She caught a glimpse of herself in the makeup mirror attached to the corner of her desk. Giving in to a childish impulse, she playfully stuck out her tongue before smiling. Starr was the image of her father, and thankfully looking like him hadn't hurt her cute factor. She maintained her light caramel complexion with lots of spa treatments, drinking plenty of water and avoiding the number-one zit magnet—chocolate. She had high cheekbones and almond-shaped eyes that slanted upward. From her mother she got her hair and her perky mouth. But mostly she was the spitting image of her father, and she loved it big-time.

Starr leaned forward to study her face for any signs of impending acne—leaving makeup on overnight was a no-no. Satisfied with her smooth complexion, she ran her slender fingers through her newly styled asymmetrical Rihanna-look-alike cut and opened her new MacBook Air laptop.

Click.

She eyed her Kimora Lee Simmons Barbie doll perched atop her crystal jewelry box. She kept the doll on display, since she had another one that her father had had signed by the Fabulous One herself. That doll was stored inside a Plexiglas collector's case on top of her fireplace mantel. Starr loved, loved, *loved* Kimora and everything about her fabulous life. She'd never had the chance to meet her, but every week Starr hosted a viewing party for Kimora's reality show, *Life in the Fab Lane*. In fact, she was secretly a member of Kimora's fan club.

Although Starr hadn't gone so far as to practice Kaballah or wear her hair hanging down to the middle of her back, she did meditate every morning, did yoga and *vowed* that just like Kimora, *she* would own the largest private collection of Louis Vuitton luggage and handbags. "One day," she promised herself aloud as she clicked her rhinestone-covered mouse.

The e-mail she'd sent her mom a few weeks back popped up on the screen. Her perfectly straight, bright-white teeth bit down softly on her lip-gloss-covered mouth as her eyes scanned the screen.

TO: HOTMAMA2001@YAHOO.COM
FROM: STARRS_WORLD@YAHOO.COM
RE: STARR'S TOP FIVE B-DAY WISHES
IMPORTANCE: CRUCIAL!!!
5. Donation in my name to a battered women's shelter or animal shelter or something like that *(it's always good to give back, right?)*
4. Rolex watch *(diamonds are a girl's best friend)*
3. Ralph Lauren crocodile Ricky bag *(the hot pink one of course)*
2. Louis Vuitton sac chien dog carrier *(The Lesters always travel in style!!)*
☺ And a drumroll please for Starr's #1 b-day wish…
1. A cute little, harmless, easy to clean after, even easier to love Yorkie *(uh, that's a Yorkshire terrier)*
Love Ya.
Starr

She wondered if they would finally cave and let her have a Yorkie. Her mother was allergic and her father complained that it would poop all over the house—both were irrelevant to Starr. Besides, she thought it was big-time gracious of her to cut the list down from ten to five—and that had been very, very hard to do. Her fifteenth birthday was major and it deserved to be celebrated in a major way. Right? Right.

Starr slipped her feet back into her favorite satin slippers—bright pink, of course—and rolled back in the chair. She knew this family dinner with Dad was big for her mom and being late was not an option with the one and only Sasha "HotMama" Lester. She had to admit to herself that she was big-time excited about it, too. She loved her dad just as much as he loved her. Most times she understood that being in the music business and his lifestyle kept him away from the family, with all the travel and late-night listening parties. That was all a part of his world, but it didn't stop her from missing him like crazy.

Ding.

Starr heard her IM alert just as she crossed the plush carpet of her bedroom floor. She stared at her laptop and then quickly shifted her eyes toward the elevator outside her bedroom door. Hoping her mother wouldn't call her again on the intercom, Starr dashed across the room and clicked the mouse to open the instant message.

MARIMARI: STARR, U THERE? I NEED HELP…BIGTIME!!!!!

It was one of Starr's best friends, Marisol Rivera. Usually, she wasn't one of those girls who blew up over nothing just to get attention, so Starr knew if Marisol said it was big-time important—then it *had* to be.

Starr dropped back down into her chair.

Rule #1 for being a Pacesetter: always be there for advice and guidance, and always be available…when it's convenient.

UR#1STARR: I'M HERE. WHADDUP?
MARIMARI: HIT OR MISS?

An image of Marisol via her Webcam popped onto the screen. Starr's eyes went straight to Marisol's smooth bronze complexion. Her long jet-black curly hair framed her doe-shaped eyes, high cheekbones and perky, lip-gloss-covered mouth. She was Dominican, and except for her long silky black hair and her hard-to-miss accent, she looked African-American. No one could deny that Mari was pretty and had a slammin' size-8 body that Starr would kill for. Life as a size 4 was no fun.

Her eyes shifted down to scrutinize Marisol's outfit. The high-waist, dark-rinse jeans she wore with the suede charcoal-gray flats went perfectly with the bright pink-gray-and-white long-sleeved fitted tee. Several long gold chain necklaces and a pink Birkin bag made the seemingly ordinary outfit look simply extraordinary. It definitely suited Marisol's glamour-girl style.

Starr's fingers flew across the keyboard.

UR#1STARR: DEFINITELY A HIT. U GET A GOLD STARR, DIVA!!
MARIMARI: ☺
UR#1STARR: SINCE THE OUTFIT IS SO CAS YOU COULD WEAR UR HAIR IN A SIDE PONYTAIL. MARIAH WORE HER HAIR LIKE THAT LAST WEEK AT OUR HOUSE.
MARIMARI: U R SO RIGHT, DIVA.

Marisol blew her a kiss just before her image disappeared from the laptop screen.

Starr sighed in disappointment. It was too bad their dress-up game was just that…a game. Pace Academy students were required to wear uniforms—really stupid-looking uniforms. The dress code consisted of a putrid-looking, pleated, tartan plaid skirt in blue and gray, a corny red cardigan or a blazer and a Peter Pan-collared, librarian-looking white blouse. No matter how much you tried to accessorize, the look spelled: *D-E-A-T-H-2-S-T-Y-L-E*.

Starr felt a little let down that Marisol hadn't asked her what her pretend first-day outfit was. Most likely because Marisol didn't think Starr needed any help, not because Mari didn't care.

She wished she could wear something from her secret stash—one drawer deep in her walk-in, mini-Kimora closet where she gave in to her hip-hop-wannabe desires—with its low-cut halters, skinny jeans and short denim skirts. No one in her family knew about the drawer because she kept it under lock and key, and she was the only one who knew where the key was hidden. She didn't even let her friends know she sometimes locked the door to her bedroom suite, pulled the ceiling-to-floor-length silk curtains closed and had a hip-hop video fashion show for her precious porcelain black doll collection. Her dad could be a little overprotective at times about what she wore. And he would never allow her to leave the house looking like she wanted to star in a video, which meant showing a little more skin and a curvier body.

Starr sighed. It was okay for him to have all those thong-wearing, strapless-dress sporting, big-booty women in his artists' videos, though. *Whateva.*

She thought about checking in on her best friend Dionne, but she decided to pass. She really wanted to put in some quality time with her dad—especially with him leaving Friday for a weekend of partying at the MTV Video Music Awards. She was annoyed that her parents had nixed her own plans for a fabulous weekend in L.A. But that didn't mean that she was going to sulk.

Starr stepped into the elevator off her bedroom suite in the three-story mansion that the Lesters had called home for the past five years. In seconds she was descending from the second floor, stepping out into the great room on the first floor.

She looked out the floor-to-ceiling windows at the acres and acres of lawn. The family hardly ever used the room that ran the length of nearly half the mansion, with two large fireplaces at either end of the room. There were three separate seating areas, but the room flowed together seamlessly. Although Starr was accustomed to its grandeur, she knew the high ceilings and opulent decor took most visitors' breath away. The room was more about elegance and showcasing wealth than comfort. Even so, she'd always thought it odd that it was the only room in the mansion that *didn't* have a television in it. Moving quickly, she made her way down the long marble-floored hallway to the dining room.

She paused in the arched doorway and was surprised. The table was set for a formal meal. Large porcelain china serving bowls filled with food were laid across a runner down the center of the huge wooden table, but no one was in the room. Starr's hand automatically went to her pavé diamond pendant just as Mimi, their live-in maid, came bustling through the door that connected the dining room to the gourmet chef's kitchen.

"Where's everybody, Mimi?" Starr asked as she stepped into the room and watched the tall, thin black woman begin gathering bowls into her arms.

Mimi looked up and her eyes were instantly apologetic. Starr knew it before the words even came out of Mimi's mouth. "Your father got a last-minute invitation to a dinner party. Your mother went with him."

Starr didn't want Mimi's pity even if it was pathetic that her parents hadn't bothered to let her know they had other plans. She held her head high and hid the pain she felt in her chest. Sometimes her parents' absence—some might say neglect—really sucked, and most times it really hurt.

"The twins are in the kitchen eating with Justine and me. Come on and have dinner with us, too."

Just what she wanted: another night with her four-year-old twin brothers from hell, Malcolm and Martin, the cook and the maid. "I'm not really hungry," she said.

Before she could protest, Starr turned and hurried from the dining room. She didn't bother with the elevator and instead ran up the marble staircase—two steps at a time—to her suite. She barely made it into her room before she flung herself onto the center of the bed and buried her head.

She didn't want to eat. She didn't want Justine and

Mimi to distract her with their stories or listen to the constant babble of the twins. She just wanted to be alone because at least that way she could hide her disappointment.

bedroom apartment that could fit inside her father's new living room. She loved Newark and all her Brick City friends. But the other side of the world where Starr and Marisol were her BFFs and she was one-third of the über-popular Pacesetters…well, she loved it more.

She *wished* she could live in that world full-time but there were three things that would have to happen:

1) Her mother and father, who only dated for three months, some sixteen odd years ago—would have to decide to get together again. *(The way they fought…uhm, that was a definite no!)* 2) Her mother would have to agree to let her only child live with her father. *(The devil had a better chance of ice-skating in hell.)* And 3) Her father would have to stay off the road long enough to agree to let her live with him. *(Humph, Daddy loves being Lahron the Don on that stage…so who knows?)*

Dressed in a fitted turquoise Polo shirt with a metallic big pony logo, Dionne checked the MAC polish on her toenails for dryness before she removed the lime-green toe separators. She studied her toes while bopping her head to the beat of Beyoncé's video on MTV Jams. The front door opened just as she hit a high note along with Mrs. B.

"Didi, what did I tell you 'bout watchin' all them dang-on videos?"

Mommy's home.

Dionne used the remote to turn the volume down so that the bass of the music didn't make the African sculptures on the wall bounce.

"Thank you," Risha Hunt called from the kitchen.

Dionne sighed, thinking about her situation as she worked the four thin gold bangles around her left wrist. Usually the bracelets brought her out of the blues. Each of the bangles was engraved with comforting words: *LOVE, FAITH, PEACE* and *STRENGTH*. They were gifts from Starr and Marisol for her fifteenth b-day this past June.

She smiled as she remembered the girls gushing to her about a mention in a fashion magazine that said Mariah Carey, Halle Berry and Jessica Simpson owned them. Dionne didn't have her own Amex like the other girls— her Moms said she was way too young—so she couldn't afford the three-thousand-dollar price tag. Heck, it took her mom two whole months to make that working at University Medical Center.

Her bracelets helped get her through a summer of only being able to see her Pacesetter friends on her webcam or on the random weekends her dad was off the road long enough for her to spend time with him in the city. Hopefully they would help her get over not being there with her dad at his very first VMAs. Her mom vetoed the whole thing because she didn't want her to miss school on Monday.

Dionne climbed off the couch and made her way into the kitchen. Her mom—who at thirty-five years old looked more like her sister—turned to look over her shoulder. "Girl, school starts tomorrow and you cooped up in this house?" she asked, leaving the wooden spoon in the pot of leftover spaghetti she was warming up for dinner. "Joshia and Kim are on their stoop."

Dionne just shrugged. Her Moms would never understand that her friendship with her ex-BFFs was soooo *finito*. Either they were carrying on like groupies about her father or they were giving her the cold shoulder because they were jealous of her new designer clothes and her trips down the red carpet or her pictures in magazines...or a gazillion other things she thought were so lame of them to get mad about. At Pace, just about *everybody* was somebody so there was none of that *"Oh, my gosh your dad is Lahron the Don"* BS.

"I am soooo ready for the first day of school," Dionne grumbled as she reached in the front pocket of her Rock & Republic jeans for the small and flat glass container holding her favorite lip gloss in sheer peach.

Risha's two pairs of gold bamboo doorknockers clanged lightly against each other as she walked over to her daughter. "Let me holla at you for a sec. Sit."

Dionne dropped down into one of the chairs surrounding the kitchen table. She wished her nails were long enough—or that she had acrylic tips—so that she could drum them against the table as she sat through what she anticipated was going to be another "Remember Where You Came From" lecture.

"Look here, girl. I'm still young enough to remember being fifteen and tryin' to be fly and all that. But don't forget where you come from...because it might be a place you have to come back to. The last thing you want waitin' for you on these here streets is haters and enemies."

Dionne began nervously twisting her bangles again as she looked dead in her mother's eyes. "We've talked about this before."

"We sure have because I don't want you to base *your* life on what your father has. If the money goes—and Lord knows that's possible with the way he spending it—then the clothes and the thirty-grand-a-year private school and all the other bling-things you didn't have a year ago will go, too."

Dionne had to fight not to roll her eyes. "Don't be a hater, Ma."

Risha laughed and it wasn't an angry laugh or a sad laugh or even a hater laugh. Just a knowing, amused laugh, like when she heard Martin Lawrence doing stand-up. A laugh like she thought her daughter was adorable. "Honey, I *never* thought I would be able to buy Cisco for a quarter."

Dionne frowned. "Who?"

"Exactly," Risha said, rising to her feet as she reached down to stroke Dionne's cheek. "I wish your daddy the best. I really do, Didi. I just don't want *you* to get hurt if *his* career doesn't work out."

Dionne nodded but deep down she was scared. What her Moms said made sense. She excused herself and walked down the long and narrow hall filled with her baby pictures until she reached her bedroom. The dark denim decor with lime-green accents did nothing to comfort her.

She opened her cramped closet and looked at the dozens of new outfits and school uniforms her father bought for her to start school with. Two years ago, her mom and dad had spent a couple hundred dollars on Macy's, Old Navy and H&M to get her clothes for the start of the school year. Now her dad paid that for one pair of designer jeans or her Marc Jacobs tie-front pointelle blouse in that to-die-for shade of madras red or seven times that for her new "don't touch it or you will pull back a nub" monogrammed Louis Vuitton Galliera tote. And *that* was just the tip of the iceberg when it came to her new wardrobe.

She thought of their shopping spree two weeks ago and the huge wad of money her father kept pulling out of his pocket, peeling off…and off…and off hundred-dollar bills at every cash register. He denied her nothing. The fleeting thought of him winding up broke passed through her mind. She scrunched up her face like she'd smelled fresh dog poo when she imagined Lahron the Don going broke blasted all over Internet blog sites—just like the scandalous news that one of the hottest stars' SUV got repo'ed a while back.

That was bad. *Big-time* bad.

three

Marisol Rivera let out a deep breath through pursed lips as she used one slender finger to tap the button to increase her treadmill speed. With Rihanna blaring through the earphones of her iPod and MTV's *My Super Sweet 16* on the small flat-screen monitor attached to the handlebars of her treadmill, Marisol closed her eyes and made sure to breathe in and out through her lip-gloss-covered mouth. *A lady should always wear makeup,* she thought.

She wanted to get in one last workout before school tomorrow. Unlike Starr and Dionne, Marisol felt like her butt was just one Twinkie away from being filled with dimples and bumps and lumps—okay maybe not *that* bad...but close. She knew Latinas—ahem, J-Lo—were well-known and envied for their derrieres...she just didn't want it to get out of hand before it was too late. *Madre de Dios,* like her *Tia* Maria.

Marisol shuddered at the thought as she finished up the last mile and then turned the treadmill off. She walked across the state-of-the-art exercise room and checked out her appearance in the mirrored wall. She liked the way the white velour Juicy Couture tracksuit fit her frame, but she wished her almost-nonexistent chest would've sprouted like her hips and her thighs. Of course, her parents wouldn't want her looking like a Coca-Cola bottle but she wasn't happy with a future as a pear, either.

"Maybe I'll ask for a personal trainer like Starr," she said aloud to herself, in her heavily Spanish-accented voice.

With a final shrug, Marisol surveyed the huge expanse of her father's exercise room. As the star pitcher for one of New York's Major League Baseball teams, Alex Rivera trained hard to stay in shape to maintain his physique *and* his celebrity. New York definitely loved her father. With his strikeout record, his good looks and his ability to charm, he always got invites to parties, appearances on late-night TV, a paparazzi following, making *People* magazine's "100 Most Beautiful" and endorsements that were beginning to rival Tiger Woods.

Next week ESPN was doing one of those day-in-the-life-of documentaries following her dad around for a whole week. Wherever he went, they went. All access, all Alex Rivera, all the time.

Papi was *muy* popular and paid.

Marisol drew on her eight years of dance training and "walked it out" across the polished wooden floors, down the hall to the staircase leading upstairs to the bedrooms. Her stomach growled and she thought about buzzing the chef to make her a sundae, but she passed. "No, Marisol," she admonished herself with a shake of her head. *"Un momento en los labios, toda una vida en mi cadera."* (Translation: A moment on the lips, a lifetime on my hips.)

She glanced down at her diamond Rolex watch—a gift from her mother. It was just a little past nine-thirty in the evening.

Marisol was glad that she didn't have a curfew like Dionne. She couldn't imagine going to bed at 10:00 p.m., especially since she was hardly sleepy then. What was there to do? Stare at the ceiling? *That* was big-time crazy.

Right about now she wanted to lounge in a hot bubble bath while she read the latest issues of her celebrity and fashion magazines. She was hoping to get some inspiration for a gift for Starr's birthday. What do you get someone who has everything?

Marisol thought of Starr's birthday wish list.

Her parents had definitely vetoed her buying Starr the dog she wanted.

She loved Starr to death, but she was not going to have to explain to her parents why she spent nearly twenty grand on the Ricky bag Starr wanted. Her parents were very generous, but she was smart enough not to push it.

And of course the Rolex was a definite no. Plus,

Marisol knew that Starr only really wanted the watch because she had one. And that gave her a bit of smug satisfaction knowing that she had *something* that *the* Starr Lester wanted.

Maybe she could convince her driver to take the three of them and a couple of PWs—Pacesetter wannabes—out for a birthday dinner at some fabulous restaurant in the city and maybe go to a club.

Marisol began to worry as she thought of all the things that could possibly go wrong with that plan: How exactly was she going to convince her driver to take her and a bunch of teenage girls to the city for a night on the town without her parents' okay? Besides, Starr was so picky about her circle of friends—meaning she and Dionne were definite BFFs, but other stylish, hip, popular girls she merely tolerated. Everyone else was a no-no.

Okay, scratch the whole multiracial version of NYC Prep, Marisol thought as she reached up to twist her highlighted hair into a loose topknot.

She paused as another thought popped into her head. She snatched her cell and quickly texted Starr.

MARIMARI: R U Having a B-Day Bash? 4 Words: MTVs Super Sweet 16.

She hit send and waited a few seconds to see if Starr would answer. When she didn't get a response she logged that topic of conversation on to their TBD (To Be Discussed) list for tomorrow.

Marisol was halfway up the stairs when she heard loud voices coming from her parents' suite at the end of the hall.

"I am sick of *your* career intruding on *my* life, Alexandro!"

Marisol winced at the anger she heard in her mother's voice. She knew that her mother didn't agree with her father's lifestyle since he became a superstar athlete. The celebrity parties, the paparazzi, the showboating—none of it suited the family-oriented, laid-back Yasmine Rivera one bit.

"As long as it pays for every aspect of your luxury lifestyle, right, Yasmine?" her father shouted in rapid-fire Spanish.

Marisol crept up the stairs on the tips of her sequined Juicy Couture sneakers—of course. They weren't really suited for exercise or any athletic activity. But when she first saw them, she fell in love with them. By the time she reached their carved wooden double doors her attention was focused back on her parents. She pulled loose strands of her hair behind her ear and then leaned in closer.

"I am tired of this, Alexandro," she heard her mother say in a low voice that scared her way more than her mother's screaming. She couldn't explain why. It just did.

Suddenly she didn't feel like eavesdropping anymore. Marisol turned and crept away from their door.

"Marisol?"

Her foot froze poised in the air at the sound of her father's deep voice. *Shoot.* She plastered a huge and bright "daddy's girl" smile on her face as she turned. Her eyes were level with his charcoal-gray silk shirt so she tilted her head back to look him in the face. His six-foot-three-inch height made her five-foot-six frame feel petite. "How was the game?" she asked.

"We won." He tilted his boyishly handsome face to the side as he slid his hands inside his dark and stylish denims. "Were you eavesdropping?" he asked.

"Definitely not," Marisol lied in a voice as if she was insulted at the very idea.

"Why don't you make sure Carlos is in bed for your mother? And don't stay up too late, Mari." Alex tugged her ponytail before walking past her to jog down the stairs.

"Daddy, are you going out?" she called out as she turned to watch him.

Alex paused on the steps. Marisol thought her father looked so handsome as the light from the chandelier illuminated the soft black curls of his hair and bronzed tint of the complexion she inherited. Her heart swelled with love for him because she was a daddy's girl and she knew she had him in the palm of her hand.

He nodded. "I have a sports-bar opening to attend."

She thought of her parents' argument. "Is Mami going?"

He shook his head. "No, you know it's not her kind of thing. I won't be out long."

Marisol wanted to say a dozen different things. Her mouth opened but nothing came out except, "'Kay."

She flicked her thumbnail against the gold band of the chunky turquoise ring she wore on her index finger. Just as the sound of the front door closing behind him echoed throughout the house, Marisol looked over her shoulder. Her mother switched off the lights in their bedroom.

She sighed as she made her way to her brother's room.

She was having a great day and pretty good night and now family drama just sucked up all her joy. On top of that she found herself sinking into a real funky mood. Before she opened the door to her eleven-year-old brother's room, she took a deep breath to keep from smelling the odor of feet, moldy plates and only God knows what else.

Marisol took a quick peek inside her brother's room, which was designed entirely around sports paraphernalia. The lights were out and there was a lump under the covers on the bed. Good enough for her.

She eased his door closed to keep him from waking up and working her nerves. Right now the soaking tub in her bathroom had her name written *all* over it.

four

Starr
September 2 @ 7:20 a.m. | Mood: Powerful

Behind the dark lenses of her designer shades as she sat in the rear of the Range Rover, Starr eyed the castle-like buildings and luxurious grounds making up Pace Academy. She couldn't wait to see Marisol and Dionne so that they could make their entrance and resume their spots as the ones to watch at the elite school—just in case anyone had lost their minds during the summer break.

Starr watched the row of Jaguars, Benzes and high-end SUVs dropping their students off at the front of the main building. Her driver, Marcus, steered the Bentley toward the area reserved for visitor parking. He knew the routine well.

Every morning all three of the Pacesetters' drivers parked there to ensure that the girls always walked into school together.

Starr double-checked her face in her Swarovski crystal-encrusted compact case. She snapped it closed just as Marcus pulled the Bentley to a stop beside Dionne's chauffeured BMW in the cutest shade of royal blue.

"Unlock the doors, Marcus," Starr said as she watched Dionne grab her book bag and climb out of the car dressed in her plaid skirt, white shirt and fitted red blazer.

CLICK.

Seconds later Dionne's car pulled away as she climbed into the rear of the Bentley with Starr. They squealed excitedly as they hugged each other close.

"Thank God summer is over," Dionne drawled, raking her fingers through her long weave with loose curls created with a rod and set so it flowed down her back and against the sides of her face softly.

Starr looked at her oddly. "Girl, please, I wish it was summer all year long. Good weather, vacays, and no school? Summer is fabulous."

"There's Marisol," Dionne squealed, turning in her seat as a silver Mercedes pulled up beside them.

The SUV barely stopped before Marisol hopped out and raced over toward them. Dionne climbed out of the vehicle and hugged Marisol close.

Starr had to admit that she was glad the three of them were back together again. They had gotten to hang out some when they weren't vacationing with their families, but she had missed the three of them all hanging out together almost every single day. The world felt so right and she didn't hide the grin that spread across her face.

"Have a good day, Miss Starr," Marcus said, bending down slightly to smile at her in the rearview mirror.

She nodded and gave him a small wave. Marcus was so in tune to her wannabe great ways, so she didn't bother with the whole "put on your hat and open my door" unless he was dropping her in front of the school. She grabbed her matching Louis Vuitton messenger bag and pocketbook before she climbed out to stand beside them.

Starr winked playfully at her crew and then became all business. "First day. Freshmen. All eyes on us? But we don't care, right?"

"Right?" Dionne and Marisol answered in unison.

"Then let's *do* this," Starr said with attitude.

The three girls all took a deep breath as they made their way up the concrete walkway to the sprawling front lawn of Pace Academy. Clusters of teens were greeting each other and many stopped to greet the Pacesetters as they breezed by.

The truth was Starr was exactly like her name. She was one of the lucky ones, one of the chosen few. When people looked at Starr they thought there was nothing in the world she didn't have or couldn't get.

But nothing could be further from the truth.

As the girls climbed the staircase leading into the school, Starr cut her eyes over to the group of teens gathered under the branches of the oak tree. All were fashionably stylish despite the uniform and each was incredibly popular.

In the midst of the group was a teenage R&B star

fresh from his summer tour, two teen actors with starring roles in popular soaps, the youngest son of a former rapper with his own hit reality show, children of politicians and a few children of entertainment lawyers, who usually were just as rich as their wealthy clients. While many of the white students at Pace were from aristocratic families or the sons and daughters of wealthy businessmen and financiers, the black students were mostly from new money—the offspring of sports stars and celebrities.

"Girls, Pace Academy has its perks," Starr said salaciously, with her eyes on Jordan Jackson.

Even wearing the corny-looking Pace uniform—blazer, gray slacks, white shirt and plaid tie—he looked so divine. Jordan looked up from his iPhone and their eyes locked as he threw her that big Kool-Aid grin that *always* made her heart stop big-time.

Starr gave him the flirty smile she and Marisol perfected in the seventh grade. While butterflies took over her stomach, she recalled the particulars she jotted down in her Crush Notebook when she first saw him at Pace Academy:

Name: Jordan "Too Fine, Must Be Mine" Jackson
Age: 16
B-Day: 2/04
Fab Cred: Son of R&B singer in megagroup Shyne. (All About U is my jam!) About to drop his own album with my Dad's label so that he can be a Tru-Starr! (I HAVE to be in his 1st video.) Drives a

pimped out Benz that is all his! (Bye-bye, Marcus, hello, riding shotgun with my Boo.)
Cute Factor: 10 (Those lips. Ahhh!)
Style Factor: 7 (Way too many hoodies.)
Hot Boyz Rank: #1...OF COURSE!!!

Jordan eased past the rest of the fellas to throw an arm around Starr's shoulders. He pulled her close for a hug and she fought the urge to snuggle her face into his smooth neck and instead inhaled a deep breath of his cologne. She tried to identify it. Warm. Spicy. Gucci. Definitely Gucci—her favorite scent.

That's a sign, she thought as she pretended to be comfortable—friendly comfortable, not girlfriend comfortable—in Jordan's arms.

"Whaddup, ladies?" he said in that husky voice that only hinted that he could sing Chris Brown or Usher out of any arena.

Uhm, uhm, uhm. Starr could only shrug, as she wished she didn't get so tongue-tied around him. A crush messed a girl up *every* time...especially when that girl was fighting hard not to let him know...at least not yet.

"Nothing much. Whaddup with you?" Dionne responded, thankfully filling in the silence.

"You know my boy Reg likes you, right?" Jordan said to Dionne as he licked his lips and shifted his arm from around Starr's shoulder to grab the straps of the book bag he wore on his back.

Starr's eyes shifted from his lips to Dionne just as she

did the kinda cute and flirty shrug Starr taught her. She would have been proud…if it wasn't Jordan's face Dionne was smiling up in.

Starr's expression changed as Heather Framer, the stepdaughter of a famous Oscar-winning actress, and her crew walked up to them wearing their uniforms Lil' Kim style. With lacy leggings under their plaid skirts, bright red high heels and unbuttoned shirts with flashes of their lace bras showing, they had managed to elevate their uniforms from classy to straight trashy.

Heather and her crew were everything Starr wasn't: extra tall, with extra-large breasts, extra makeup, extra everything. They were video vixens in training.

Starr turned up her nose in distaste as she tried to arch her back to push her A-cups forward in her La Perla padded bra. She had no doubt that the whole crew were going to wind up in the headmaster's office before lunch. "Nelly is just waiting to run a credit card down the crack of someone's butt," she drawled as she studied her manicured nails.

Dionne laughed.

Marisol pursed her lips and made a face like "ohnoshedidn't."

Heather shifted uncomfortably where she stood and actually tried to ease her shirt closed a bit. "Hi, Starr."

Starr fought not to roll her eyes.

Heather was *desperate* to belong. Last year her dad, who had been a yard man, married into money. Heather's status was so precarious that if her father got divorced, he'd be back at his $11.00/hour gardening job the next day. Rumor had it that she had already done the *do* with several boys at school, including Hunter Grant—the former star of some ABC Friday-night sitcom now in syndication. Her desperation made her sleep with random guys, dress like a working girl and take whatever crap high school *It* girl, Starr Lester, dished out.

Starr actually felt a little bit sorry for her. Pace could be big-time intimidating—especially for someone who hadn't grown up with money. Behind her shades, Starr's eyes shifted to Dionne. Thankfully she took in all the newness in stride—*with* Starr's help. Unfortunately for Heather, BFF slots on the roster of Starr's closest and dearest friends were filled.

"Hi," Starr finally said, ignoring the surprised expressions on Dionne and Marisol's face.

"You workin' that uniform, Miss Heather," Jordan drawled before he licked his lips and raised one of her hands high to twirl her slowly like a showroom car on display.

In Starr's mind if Heather was a car, she would be a rusty, beat-down, hooptee with a flashy paint job that couldn't hide all the wear and tear.

Starr slipped her arms through Marisol and Dionne's to gently guide them along inside the building. Jordan had definitely just worked her last nerve and dropped down several notches on her Pace Academy Hot Boyz ranking. *Boys can be soooooooooo stupid,* Starr thought as they continued their strut up the brick-paved walkway.

"I'll holla at y'all later...*especially* you, Starr," he called out after they turned to walk away.

Mad at him or not, Starr's heart still raced as she stepped inside the doors of Pace Academy.

IT'S ON!
Posted in *uncategorized* on September 02 @ 6:00 a.m. by thedivaofdish
Today is the very first day of school at ole Pace Academy. Not exactly sure how I really feel. I mean I love Pace Academy and all, but the freaky teachers? Mr. Funky-breath, the Headmaster? Silly classes? Insignificant grades? Horrible rules? Terrible school lunches? Wannabe cliques? Gross drama?
Puh-leeze.
In one hour we all fill the halls and the school year begins. What will it bring? What will go down? What will I have to say about it all? Check back often and peep Pace Academy...the way I see it.
Just remember this is for students' eyes only. So don't tell. Just in case you all can't keep a secret, I'll show you that I can fo sho, because who I really am is for me to know and you all not to bother trying to find out!
Smooches,
Pace Academy's Diva of Dish

0 comments

five

Dionne
September 2 @ 7:40 a.m. | Mood: Grateful

walking inside the main hall of Pace Academy was like stepping back in time. The long tiled hallway. The front of the lockers covered with dark walnut doors. The eighteen-foot ceilings arched like cathedrals. The floors smelled like polishing wax and the paneling and railings had a lemon-scented fragrance from what the cleaner used on the wood throughout the building.

Depending on the lighting, Pace Academy could look as heavenly as a church or as creepy as a haunted house. Well, to Dionne anyway. *It was a long, long way from South 17th Street Elementary.*

She remembered how afraid she had been last year when she walked inside the main hall that very first day. Everything was so different—so new, so scary. Even though there were three hundred students at Pace, Dionne had been scared. *Thank God I have Marisol and Starr with me now,* she thought to herself as she twisted her precious bracelets.

"Welcome back to Pace Academy," Marisol said softy, as they stood there framed by the sunlight beaming in from the open doors behind them.

Time seemed to stand still as the activity around them moved in slow-motion as they tried to take it in. All eyes were on them. It was as if now, school could officially start. The Pacesetters had arrived. The girls loved it. Starr couldn't have planned a better entrance.

"Too bad classes and teachers have to go along with all this," Dionne whispered as if she wasn't still overwhelmed by their popularity. She pulled her vibrating Sidekick from her purse and slid it open with a flick of her thumb.

Starr just gave a hint of a smile as she stepped up to the large display board and pushed her shades atop her asymmetrical haircut. "There's a freshmen assembly right after homeroom," she told them as they stepped up behind her.

"Good, my first-period class is algebra." Marisol's high-pitched voice was agitated. "I mean no offense, but how is that going to teach me how to handle my inheritance one day? Seriously? Seriously? Se-ri-ous-ly!"

Dionne laughed along with Starr, but thought about what her mom had said and her life back in Newark, where most people didn't have much money.

Why couldn't her mom get back with her dad? she

thought. Or let her live with him? Or let him buy her a bigger house in a better neighborhood like he'd offered? It would be so much easier that way. Then she wouldn't have to lie to her friends.

Dionne fell back behind her friends a bit as they made their way down the hall. Starr and Marisol knew she lived with her Moms. But they thought Risha Hunt was a stay-at-home mom, living off a stipend from Dionne's father in a huge house in Livingston, New Jersey, who was busy with lots of charity work. She only hung out with them or had weekend sleepovers at her dad's apartment. They didn't know anything about her real life with her mom in Newark in a two-bedroom apartment. They didn't realize her mother had to work. They didn't know about her old Newark friends or her crush, Hassan—none of it. She always had to stay on her toes and keep her story straight to keep her friends from finding out.

Dionne thought of the text message her Moms had just sent her:

DIDISMOM: GOOD LUCK ON YOUR 1ST DAY. XOXO.

She pushed aside her guilt as she followed her friends into the girls' bathroom on the first floor at the end of the brightly lit, long hallway. Yet again, something as simple as a place to go to the bathroom was so different from her old life. There was no institutional gray-colored tile, prisonlike sink troughs lining the wall or bathroom stalls with the faint scent of industrial-strength ammonia.

Pace Academy's bathrooms had a plush waiting area with two chaise longues upholstered in suede, marble-tiled floors throughout and wood-framed mirrors above pedestal sinks. The stalls were white with enough room to comfortably change clothes. Floral arrangements were positioned around the huge vanity area and the walls had a mural of some garden-of-Eden-looking scene. Crystal chandeliers hung from the ceilings. And the faint scent of something sweet and fruity hung in the air.

There was a trio of floor-length mirrors in the corner that provided a 360-degree view of one's outfit. Small wooden boxes contained pads and tampons for those "special" days that every girl hates.

It was not like any school bathroom Dionne had ever seen. Indeed, nothing at Pace Academy was like anything she had ever seen.

Starr reached in her messenger bag and pulled out an OUT OF ORDER sign. She stepped outside and stuck it on the door of the bathroom. She kept one handy for times like this when they needed some privacy.

Dionne checked her hair in the mirror while Marisol flopped down onto one of the chaise longues.

"Just a quick FYI before we head to homeroom," Starr told them as she moved across the floor and dropped her purse and messenger bag next to Marisol.

"Last night I decided that I want a huge birthday party and I want it to be on MTV's *My Super Sweet 16*," Starr declared as if she was announcing that she was running for president.

"Liar, liar," Marisol muttered under her breath.

Starr ignored her.

Dionne watched their reflections in the mirror.

"It's going to be one of the best—no, correction—*the* best Sweet Sixteens!"

"But you're going to be *fifteen*," Marisol stressed as she flipped her hair over her shoulder and applied lip gloss to her lips.

Starr whipped around to eye her and cocked an eyebrow really high. "No sugar-honey iced tea, Sherlock."

Marisol shrugged.

Dionne bit back a smile.

Most of the time, Marisol and Starr quietly struggled with each other to see just who was in charge. It was during those tugs-of-war and silly moments that Dionne just sat back and enjoyed the show.

Starr rolled her eyes at Mari and began to pace up and down the length of the bathroom. The stiffness of her uniform skirt made a *swishing* noise as she moved. "There are only a few more weeks and there is a lot of planning to do. I don't know why I didn't think of this sooner."

Marisol snorted and muttered something under her breath that Dionne didn't catch. She eyed her. Marisol gestured that she would tell her about it later. Dionne's guess was that the whole B-day bash was Marisol's idea and not Starr's. Their friend had a way of claiming an idea as her own.

"I'll have my mom's party planner put it all together

and Daddy will contact MTV and get *that* ball rolling." Star continued to pace and the *swishing* seemed to get louder.

There was no stopping Starr Lester when she was on a mission.

The first bell rang.

Dionne grabbed her book bag. "I'm out, y'all," she told them over her shoulder before she walked out the bathroom. She wanted to get to class on time. After her talk with her mom last night she was keenly aware that Pace Academy with its high price tag and fancy bathroom was more of a blessing than a right.

SIX

Marisol
September 02 @ 11:43 a.m. | Mood: Nosy

MARISOL'S ponytail bobbed up and down at the back of her head as she walked as fast as she could without drawing too much attention to herself. Her eyes scanned the crowd of rowdy students. All one hundred and thirty upperclassmen ate lunch during the same period: 12:30 p.m. The Pace Academy dining hall resembled an upscale mall food court, with most of the students lined up at one of the various food stations.

Mari's stomach growled at the thought of tasting a pepperoni personal-pan pizza from the pizza station, but she ignored the hunger pangs and forged ahead. Starr and Dionne were walking toward their table with large frozen fruit cups. Marisol headed straight for them.

"Guess what?" she gasped, still trying to catch her breath after her mini-sprint across campus.

Starr sat down in one of the chairs surrounding the large round wooden table. She frowned at Marisol's attire—a *very* fitted unitard. "Is that a camel toe?" she asked, eyeing the wedge between Marisol's thighs.

"Why you looking so hard, Starr?" Marisol snapped, even as she whipped her gym bag in front of her body.

"It was pretty hard to miss," Starr volleyed back as she stirred the smoothie with her straw.

"An-y-way…there's a blog about Pace Academy. Everyone was talking about it in gym class," Marisol told them as she reached for Dionne's cup and took a deep slurp. She frowned at the taste of mango as she passed it back to Didi. She *hated* mangos.

Starr sighed like she was bored.

Dionne took a deep swallow of her smoothie.

Oh, no they didn't, Marisol thought. She was not one to be ignored. She dropped her duffel bag on top of the table and dug her hand inside its side pocket to pull out her BlackBerry. She cleared her throat and licked her pouty lips. "Only half the school day is gone and the drama is already flying as thick as Tyra Banks's weave."

Marisol averted her eyes and when she looked back at her friends she was more than a little satisfied to find their eyes on her. They all loved juice and the best was yet to come.

Starr reached up to grab Marisol's phone but Marisol stepped back out of her reach with a wicked *na-nana-na-na* smile.

Marisol continued on. "What heiress to her mommy's

makeup fortune—and resident Paris Hilton wannabe—
returned to good old Pace with less nose than she left with
last June? Looks like she spent her summer 'refreshing' her
face. Careful, sweetie, Little Kim had to start somewhere…"

"No!" Starr gasped in shock as she slammed her hand
on the tabletop and rose to her feet. "Kylie Kilnon or
Margaret Asner?"

Marisol cleared her throat again and read on. "No
need to guess. The divaofdish is bringing it to you straight
with no chaser. Check out the before-and-after pics below
hot off the press," Marisol read with satisfaction.

Dionne reached over to yank Marisol down onto one
of the chairs around their table. The three friends strained
their necks to eye Marisol's screen.

"Kylie Kilnon," they all said in unison.

All three heads swung to the right as their eyes zoomed
in on Kylie and her crew of Paris/Lindsay/Nicole wannabes huddled around the tables of the members of the
varsity basketball team. They hadn't even noticed any
change in her, but then the cheerleaders and jocks were
definitely not on their social radar.

"Forget her and her new nose," Starr insisted, drawing
their eyes back to her. "Who's the blogger?"

"No one knows." Marisol loosened her ponytail and
then finger-combed her hair.

Now that she raced straight from gym with her news
she was very aware of her appearance in the crowded
dining hall. Juicy gossip was momentarily pushed to the

back burner as she dug her gold Chanel compact from her purse. "A lot of people are nervous. This blog takes being 'talked about'—" Marisol did the air quotes "—to a whole 'nother level. Crucial."

"Definitely," Starr and Dionne agreed before taking long slurps of their fruit smoothies.

Marisol used her key to unlock the massive mahogany door to the house. She barely nudged the door open when something stopped her, causing her to walk face-first into the door. She fixed her face into a frown and pushed against the door again with her shoulder.

"Ow!"

The holler of pain gave her eyes an extra twinkle—especially when the door was suddenly jerked from her hand. Her complaints evaporated from her lips as she slowly tilted her head up to look into the face of what had to be the *finest* hot boy ever. He looked to be seventeen or eighteen years old. Marisol's "HOW TO FLIRT 101" went into full effect: tilt the head, lick the glossy lips just so and smile (with your mouth and your eyes). *Thank God I changed out of those funky-looking gym clothes,* she thought.

"Hi," she greeted him softly as her eyes peeped his game.

He was tall and just as deliciously fine—even down to the light spray of freckles across his nose. His hair was cut low in a buzz and it only made his dimples even more deliciously deep.

She smiled.

He smiled back.

One LUV CONNECTION coming up.

Cute Stranger

+ Marisol

—————————

Love 4Ever

"Corey!"

Her new crush whirled around and it was *then* that Marisol finally noticed that the foyer of their house was filled with camera equipment and plenty of jeans-and-T-shirt-clad people and her dad...and they all were looking over at them!

Marisol swiped a strand of hair behind her ear and played it cool even though she felt her entire body flush from her high cheekbones down to the French pedicure on her toenails.

Embarrassing, she thought.

She'd been caught flirting with a cutie big-time.

"Is that thing on?" Marisol asked, pointing a dainty finger at one of the two cameras pointed in their direction.

Suddenly a huge bright light shone on her face.

"It is now," someone said loudly.

Marisol immediately shook away any creepy flatness from her hair and gave the camera her very best *America's Next Top Model* pose.

She was a natural!

seven

Dionne
September 5 @ 6:45 p.m. | Mood: Excited

DIONNE was the last of the three to walk into Starr's suite and that's because the lavishness always…always… always took her aback. The apartment where she lived with her mom was dwarfed in size by Starr's bedroom suite. One year into their friendship and she still couldn't believe it, conceive of it, nor was she ever going to achieve it.

Puh-leeze.

It wasn't her usual weekend with her dad—he was in L.A. VMAing it, but her mom felt bad enough about nixing her VMA plans that she let her spend the whole weekend at Starr's. This weekend she would be right there for all the fabulous festivities. She absolutely *hated* those Mondays when Starr and Marisol wanted to fill her in on all she missed during the sleepover: the tasty treats, the deluxe spa treatments in her personal salon, the gossip, the boy talk. And of course the hours spent playing dress-up in Starr's parents' closet.

All of it.

Well, she wasn't going to miss any of the fabulous-ness…this time.

Dionne covered her awestruck feelings well though, as she strolled in like this life of luxury was something she was used to. The girls all dropped their bags carrying the spoils from their trip to the mall next to their book bags underneath Starr's desk. The first week of school was behind them. They were all good students, but there was no need to ruin a perfectly good weekend with home-work from school. *Seriously.*

Starr kicked off her Gucci shoes before she strutted across the plush carpeting to her walk-in closet. She flung the double doors open and the large interior of the closet was immediately bathed in soft light making it look like a high-end fashion boutique. One entire wall was filled with shelves filled with perfectly folded rows of jeans, and sweaters, T-shirts and accessories that filled dark brown wicker baskets.

She headed straight for one of the baskets and pulled out three pairs of flip-flops. She slipped on the bubble-gum pink ones, tossed the lemony-yellow pair to Marisol and the coconut-white ones to Dionne. "Heels. Can't live with them, won't live without them," she grumbled as she flip-flopped her way back across the room to her desk.

"Tell me about it," Dionne agreed, as she gladly kicked off her own shoes for the soft, padded cushiness of the flip-flops. "I was a Reebok and Nike vandal before I met you two."

"You're welcome," Marisol drawled.

Dionne flipped her the bird.

"Countdown to Kimora, ladies," Starr called over to them after logging off of her laptop. She walked over to the double doors on the far wall of her bedroom.

Usually they watched reruns of the oh-so-fab Kimora on Sunday nights. But the VMAs definitely preempted Kimora.

Dionne wiggled her toes freely before rising to her feet as Starr flung the doors open wide. In Dionne's mind the doors to heaven were opened as Starr's very own personal movie theater was revealed. There was plenty more of her signature pink carpeting. Twelve plush leather recliners were positioned in a semicircle around a pale gold curtain-covered wall. The entire rear of the room held a concession stand filled with all their favorite snacks—healthy and not so healthy. Behind the bar was a drink dispenser of frosty, fruity, virgin drinks. There were hot dogs, gourmet popcorn, frozen ice cream bars and bonbons. Just like a real movie theater. It was a teenager's dream.

"Don't we just love Mimi?" Starr sighed as she dug right into a glass jar filled with her favorite candy, Goobers. It was Mimi's job to make sure Starr's movie theater was fully stocked and ready for her guests.

Dionne and Marisol "big upped" in agreement before they grabbed their own pink trays, stenciled with a star, to get some treats.

Starr moved to the recliner in the center with her name engraved on the headrest. She shifted the tray attached to the side of the chair into place before sitting her goodies on it. She grabbed the remote control from the small pocket on the other side of her chair.

Just as Dionne and Marisol took seats on opposite sides of their host the familiar strains of the catchy theme song played loudly around them from the Bose sound system.

"The fabulous, fabulous..." the girls sang along as Kimora's image filled the 120-inch widescreen flat-panel TV.

Dionne wasn't as much of a fan of Kimora Lee Simmons as Starr was, but she enjoyed watching her reality show...*especially* at Starr's. She sank deep down into her recliner and took a big bite of her hot dog and a huge slurp of her drink.

This was the life.

"The fabulous, fabulous..."

Dionne couldn't agree more.

eight

Starr
September 7 @ 8:15 p.m. | Mood: Hating

starr couldn't be-*lieve* that she was watching the VMAs from the front row of her screening room and not live with her parents in L.A. Plus she got stuck babysitting her brothers. *Life sucks right now.*

"Taylor Swift looks cute," Marisol said, from her spot lying on the floor.

Starr rolled her eyes heavenward.

"I still can't believe Kanye," Dionne said, before shoving a mouthful of Goobers into her mouth.

Starr sighed.

Dionne clapped excitedly as she lounged next to Starr. "Ohmygod! Your mom looks gorgeous, Starr."

Starr cut her eyes toward the screen just as her mom flipped her shoulder-length hair over her tattooed shoulder. Sasha was the ex-R&B-singer-turned-wife of music mogul Cole Lester, who was already used to living the high life as a star in her own right. She made sure that her kids lived the good life right along with her.

"Ow!" Marisol exclaimed, reaching behind her to rub her derriere through the smooth terry cloth of her Juicy Couture robe. Her mouth dropped open in shock as she eyed Malcolm—or was it Martin?—innocently standing over her with a huge grin on his face and his pudgy little fingers still poised for another pinch.

Starr hopped up to her feet and marched across the plush carpeting, barely missing stepping on Marisol's head, to scoop her little brother into her arms. "Puh-leeze stop acting like a perv, Martin."

"But I'm Malcolm," he protested in the cutest little voice.

Starr placed him in the theater seat next to hers, before she turned around just in time to see his brother reach up and pull the entire jar of jelly beans down over his head.

"Uh-oh," Dionne said gloomily from behind her.

Starr felt like crying from the *utter* injustice of it all. "Don'tyoueatoffthatfloor!" she screamed in a high-pitched tone as she pointed her finger at him and stomped her foot in frustration.

"Look, there's your dad, Dionne!" Marisol exclaimed.

Starr was too busy scolding Martin—or was it Malcolm?—in her arms to see Lahron the Don, Dionne's father. She was confident she wasn't missing much but the usual grills, shades, platinum and diamond jewelry and sagging jeans the artists favored.

As her friends continued to ooh and aah over all the celebs, Starr sat in between her twin nightmares wondering if a big spoonful of cough medicine would bring on beddy-bye just a little bit quicker.

"Starr, we love you," Malcolm (or Martin) said as he leaned forward to press a wet kiss to her arm.

"We love you, Starr," Martin (or Malcolm) agreed before he made her other arm sticky with a kiss.

"Awwwww," Marisol and Dionne said in syrupy unison.

Starr looked from one doe-eyed cutie to the other and felt her heartstrings tug. She kissed her index and middle fingers before she pressed them to each of their cheeks. "I love you, too," she told them.

"Awwwww," Marisol and Dionne chorused again.

Starr wasn't crazy. She knew it wouldn't be long before the twin terrors' good behavior and affection would be behind them, and they would start to work her nerves again. But for now she decided to enjoy the moment.

nine

Starr
September 9 @ 6:40 p.m. | Mood: Agitated

"Relax, Starr, relax."

Starr rolled her eyes before settling on her pink-and-white acrylic-covered pedicured toes. Feeling her Pilates instructor Kante's hand press gently on the small of her back, she bent down until her buttocks were in the air. He bent over to check her form and Starr fought the desire to blast a seriously malodorous fart into his almost-pretty-enough-to-be-a-girl face. She bit back a giggle.

Exercise was definitely a "to do" but that didn't stop it from making her anxious. If it wasn't for the fact that Kante was sweeter than a thousand bags of jelly beans and had a "partner" named Jackson, Starr would seriously worry about his closeness during their sessions. Dating older boys (ahem, anyone twenty and over) was one thing her parents didn't have to worry about. Starr didn't do old. She didn't even like vintage designer clothing. Secondhand armpit sweat? Definitely a "don't."

"Okay, Starrlet, one last deep breath and rise slowly to reach for the sky, sweetie," Kante said in his soft voice that was almost a whisper.

Starr did as she was instructed, opening her eyes just as she raised her slender arms high above her head. She winced at the tension all across her shoulders.

"You'd be a lot more comfortable and at ease, sweetie, if you didn't have a wedgie as deep as the line for free cheese in the hood," Kante drawled from behind her.

Starr whipped her head around to glare at him. If looks could kill, the tall and slender, baldheaded black man with the really soft-pink-and-icky glossy lips would drop like a roach in a losing battle with Black Flag. "Since it's bothering you like it's jammed up *your* butt let me correct that for you," she said sarcastically as she stared him dead in the eye and pulled out the wedgie with her index finger and thumb.

Her thong went *POP* as it slapped against her hip when she released it.

"Whaddup, Starr."

She made an ugly face filled with dismay at the sound of the voice coming from the door of the solarium. Not even closing her eyes and doing a quick count to five could get her together enough to recover from being seen digging out a wedgie…by Jordan.

Kante just flung his headband back, licked his lips that

were way more glossy than even Starr's and laughed like a hyena as he began to gather his equipment. Kante and Starr definitely had a love-hate relationship that was way more love than anything. Most times they loved sparring with each other and right now Kante was enjoying the joke on her. *Bet I can erase that Kool-Aid smile with one word. FIRED,* she thought.

Starr plastered on her best fake smile and turned to find Jordan leaning ever so slightly in the doorway with his eyes—those eyes—on her. He looked delicious in the camel-colored leather racing jacket he wore over a white tee and dark jeans. He looked good and he knew it. Starr absolutely *loved* his confidence. "Hi, Jordan," she said calmly, like her heart wasn't beating a mile a minute and her stomach didn't feel as busy as a mall on a Saturday afternoon.

"*S-V-F,* baby. *S-V-F,*" Kante said over his shoulder with a smug expression on his face as he headed toward the door. "See you Monday, Starrlet."

Starr smiled at the way Jordan stepped away from the door as Kante passed him switching like he was using his butt to sweep the floor.

"What's *SVF?*" Jordan asked, as he walked over to help her pick up and roll her exercise mat.

"Nothing," Starr lied as she picked up one end of the mat and Jordan grabbed the other. She didn't have the heart to tell him it stood for So Very Fine.

"Your party is the talk around Pace," he said, stepping closer to her with each roll of the cushy mat.

She flipped her bangs out of her face as she looked up at him. "Really," she answered, feeling her usual tongue-tied self around the cutie.

It was hard to think when each of his steps surrounded her deeper and deeper into the deliciously divine scent of Gucci Rush.

Jordan was the only boy who made her feel like their chemistry was just as powerful and crazy explosive as fireworks blasting off. Right now, she could care less about his flirting with Heather on the first day of school. Besides, he wasn't her boyfriend...yet.

Their fingers brushed as he handed her the mat and took one last step forward to stand just inches from her.

Needing space and feeling way too nervous in his presence, Starr stepped back. His hands covered hers quickly. They felt warm.

Starr felt like she could literally throw up. Why couldn't boys be as simple as hooking up a banging outfit with just the right accessories?

"I *know* I'm invited?" he asked as he did an LL-like lick of his lips.

She nodded as words escaped her.

Say something, Starr. Say something...

Smart.

Flirty.

Cool.

Funny.

Witty.

Teasing.

Just…say…anything!

Okay, anything but "I love you, Jordan Jackson, future superstar, and I want to get married as soon as we're legal. We'll be the next young, black and fabulous power couple. I'll be the Beyoncé to your Jay-Z."

Anything but that! That was way, way, way too much information.

"Oh, no, Jordan. Save all that sex appeal for your future fans…and not my daughter."

They both jumped apart a bit and looked over toward the door as Starr's dad, Cole, strolled in with a grin on his handsome face. Jordan's father, Deshante, lead singer of the platinum-selling group Shyne, stepped into the room behind him.

Both men had on enough diamonds to blind a small town. They were the epitome of black, rich and famous. No suits, unless necessary. Designer jeans, crisp white tees, funky military-style jackets, custom-made shoes.

Starr loved her daddy's style. There was never an embarrassing "what does my daddy have on?" moment. Of course he had one of the top stylists on his payroll *and* his speed dial. Whether he was chilling around the crib or strolling down the red carpet, Daddy Lester *always* represented well for the forty-and-fine crew.

Deshante pushed his shades atop his smooth bald head. "You know if they get married the tab for the wedding is all you, father of the bride."

Jordan shook his head before dropping it in his hand.

"As long as pretty boy over there knows to keep his

hands off until after the wedding," Cole said, pointing toward Jordan playfully.

"Daddy!" Starr whined, completely embarrassed. Parents knew how to make something crucial when it didn't have to be.

Starr quickly snatched up the rest of her exercise gear into one of her Louis duffel bags. After slinging it over her shoulder, she avoided Jordan's teasing brown eyes and walked up to her father with her hand out. "Tonight, me and Mama are going to look for my dresses for my party," she said. "It's in two weeks, ya know."

Cole slipped one of his hands from the pockets of his jacket to slap her hand like a high five. "Roll out. See you when you get back."

Starr arched her brow and pursed her lips before she said, "Daddy, may I please have money to buy my dresses for my parties?"

"Now there you go," he said, with a huge grin showing off the veneers that her mom made him get.

Starr fought not to roll her eyes. What was the purpose of the whole "ask me nicely" hoopla when she *knew* he was going to give her the money regardless? Just crazy.

My parents can trip when they want to.

He pressed the black Amex into her hand and Starr smiled sweetly and wiggled her fingers.

"Boy, she really looks like her mama now," Deshante teased.

"Tell me about it," Cole drawled, reaching in his pocket to pull out a wad of folded hundred-dollar bills.

He peeled off ten and put them on top of the credit card still in Starr's outstretched hand.

"You're the one who taught me to never leave the house without cash *and* credit," she reminded him, before strutting out of the room like *she* paid the hefty mortgage.

Starr fought the urge to sneak one last peek at Jordan. He really was yummy to look at...and probably even more yummy to kiss. No doubt his kiss was nothing at all like the innocent peck on the cheek she got from Hairy Harry when she was six. Or the icky grossness of Cheetos-breath Bubble-Butt Bobby when she was ten. Or the wetness of Gunther the Grabber when she was thirteen.

Kissing Jordan would be soft and sweet and tasty. It would be perfect and that's why she was determined it would go down on the night of her birthday party. Of course, *that* she would do out of range of MTV's *My Super Sweet 16* cameras. That was her business and hers alone. Holla.

"Starr."

She turned in the doorway, her cheeks still warm from the thought of her first kiss with Jordan. "Yes?"

"MTV can't do the party," Cole told her as he slipped his cell phone back onto the clip.

No!

Starr felt like the rug was being yanked from underneath her.

"Their production crews are already taping a show that week."

No! No! No!

She had already *told* people her party was going to be on MTV!

Cole eyed his daughter like he felt the storm brewing inside her. "They will definitely tape your *My Super Sweet 16* next year, baby girl, and trust me we will do it big," he offered.

"Shoot," Starr said in lieu of the real bomb she would love to screech. She forced a smile as tight as a Botoxed forehead.

Starr wanted to flip. She wanted to cry, pout, shout and turn this mother out. She wanted to demand that her daddy make it right just like always. But not in front of Jordan and his father. Later. Definitely a "to do."

ten

Dionne
September 10 @ 8:30 a.m. | Mood: Confused

DIONNE looked up from taking notes in algebra class to find Mrs. Kingsley's short frame headed her way. She hoped the portly woman was headed for Rocksy Reynolds sitting directly behind her.

"Miss Hunt, report to the headmaster's office," Mrs. Kingsley whispered to her in her British accent, almost as strong as the smell of coffee on her breath.

Dionne felt the eyes of the other seven students on her as she slid back her chair and grabbed her book bag to sling over her shoulder. Dionne notched her head high and made her way toward the solid wooden door.

"See you at lunch, Dionne."

She looked down over her shoulder to see Reggie Monton smiling up at her with all of his chocolate cuteness—dimples and all. Even the ugliness of the uniform's red blazer couldn't knock him down on the Hot Boyz rank.

"You know my boy Reg likes you, right?"

In that moment as her eyes locked with Reggie's she remembered Jordan's words clearly.

He was big-time fine and his father played for the Nets.

Still in Dionne's eyes—and heart—he was no Hassan. But Hassan was OUT and she needed a boy who was IN.

She gave him a glossy smile before she kept it moving out the classroom and down the hall. With Reggie flashing his dimples at her she didn't have time to think about why Headmaster Payne wanted to see her.

Dionne's black Gucci loafers barely made a sound on the polished tile floor or the steps as she made her way to the main hall on the first floor. She looked through the glass as she opened the door, offering a hesitant smile to Miss Lyon who lived up to her name with her massive, tightly curled red hair surrounding her chubby face.

"Have a seat, Miss Hunt."

Dionne did, pulling her book bag into her lap as she looked around at the office that looked more like a nicely furnished living room. She would play with her side ponytail some and then switched to playing with her bracelets as she fought off her nerves.

"You can go in now, Miss Hunt," Miss Lyon said from behind her wooden desk as she set the phone down.

A dozen questions ran through Dionne's mind as she made her way back to the headmaster's office.

Am I in trouble?
What did I do?
Will I get expelled?
Does that mean I have to go to Westside High?
Goodbye, Pacesetters. Hello...WHAT?
This is big-time crucial.

Dionne knocked once on the solid oak double doors leading into Headmaster Payne's office.

"Come in."

Dionne opened one of the doors and walked in. *Wow, he really has a lot of books,* she thought as she took her seat and primly crossed her ankles.

"Miss Hunt, we have been unable to contact your father regarding a serious matter—"

Dionne's heart pounded. "Did I do something wrong?" she asked, feeling like her heart was about to take a one-way cruise up her throat.

Headmaster Payne shook his head and Dionne tried not to notice that his stiff toupee shifted just a bit. Not much. But some. "Not at all," he assured her.

That made Dionne feel a *little* better.

"It's concerning your tuition. I'm sure it's just an oversight on your father's part. And...if not, unfortunately the deadline for applying for tuition assistance has passed."

Okay, that made Dionne feel big-time bad and she wished that she could shrivel into a little ball and roll out of his office from shame.

"We know your parents aren't together." Headmaster

Payne shook his head with a look of pity. "We didn't have any contact information for your mother on file."

Dionne frowned a bit as he pushed two huge manila envelopes toward her with one finger that felt like it was pointing at her accusingly.

You owe us.

You better pay us.

You don't belong.

"Please give one to your mother and the other to your father."

Dionne avoided his eyes as she grabbed the envelopes and quickly shoved them into her book bag.

"That's all, Miss Hunt."

With that her tuition-owing behind was dismissed.

Em-bar-a-sssssing.

She avoided eye contact with Miss Lyon as she scurried past her desk like a rat.

The bell rang, signaling the end of the period, but Dionne didn't head to her next class or her locker or even to find Starr and Marisol.

Dionne zoomed through the hallway filling up with students headed to the first-floor bathroom. It was funny that even with the sound of students' voices that mingled together like background noise, she could clearly hear the light ding of her bracelets hitting against each other.

LOVE, FAITH, PEACE and *STRENGTH.*

She needed all that and much, much more.

Dionne barely released her breath as she slammed inside one of the stalls and locked it. She dropped down onto the toilet seat and used shaking hands to yank her father's manila envelope out of her book bag. She tore into it—knowing she could get away with opening it. Her eyes and mouth widened bit by bit as she read the letter, silently mouthing the words that sealed her fate.

Her mother's words of advice had *never* seemed so clear:

I don't want you to base your life on what your father has. If the money goes—and Lord knows that's possible with the way he spending it—then the clothes and the thirty-grand-a-year private school and all the other bling-things you didn't have a year ago will go, too.

Her father had until the end of next week to pay her tuition or it was definitely deuces to Pace Academy and that meant deuces to Starr, Marisol and her semi-fabulous life.

eleven

Starr
September 10 @ 11:30 a.m. | Mood: Vengeful

starr was the queen of perfection.

Her boring uniform was perfectly pressed.

Her asymmetrical bob was perfectly coiffed and gleaming.

Her MAC lip gloss had her lips shining…as she kept her fake smile perfectly in place.

Starr cleared her throat as she stepped up from her spot between Dionne and Marisol to claim the mic at the center of the stage lit by a huge spotlight shaped like a star—of course. Where else would it be for *the* Starr?

Starr glanced over her shoulder at her party planner, Kyra Stone, standing off in the wings hidden by the long, cascading drapes. Starr gave her a look like "You better not screw this up."

Kyra had handled both big-bash parties and small,

intimate gatherings for her father and his closest celeb friends and business associates. She had been her mother and Starr's first choice for making sure that Starr had a party to top all parties.

Starr faced the three hundred students filling the seats of the auditorium. "Attention everyone. Attention," Starr said into the mic as she grabbed it with her perfectly manicured Crush on You red nails.

Almost as soon as she said it everyone settled down just...like...that.

"Thank you all for coming to my invite party for my Fashionista Fifteen Paaaaarrrrtyyyy!" she yelled into the mic.

Her smile became more genuine as everyone started applauding and jumped up to their feet yelling.

Starr held up her hands and motioned for them to quiet down again. "If you all would look under your seat you'll find your invitations to my party/fashion show!"

Commotion broke out as everyone in the auditorium scurried to reach under their seats for the star-shaped gift box that was filled with plenty of swag—including iPods filled with her favorite playlist and several unreleased tracks from some of her father's bestselling artists, hundred-dollar gift cards to five of her favorite design- ers, the newest makeup for girls and designer shades for the boys, a five-year subscription to each of her favorite mags and lastly...

"Since I'm cutting into your lunchtime I thought I'd

provide some gourmet pizza and a little lunchtime entertainment courtesy of TopStarr Records!"

As the doors to the auditorium opened up and waiters strolled in with personal pan-size gourmet pizza and fruit smoothies, Starr stepped back as the star-shaped spotlight disappeared and the stage darkened. When the stage lit up again, her father's top-selling artist Reign bounced onto the stage and began singing his number-one hit, "King Me."

The students forgot about their lunch as they flew up to the front of the stage.

"This is nice, Starr, and it's just the party invite," Marisol whispered to her before grabbing her hand to squeeze tightly in excitement. Dionne looked preoccupied but Starr didn't have time to wonder why.

She was too busy pretending to be perfectly pleased by the official start of her party festivities, while the whole time she was big-time pissed that none of this would be on television.

twelve

Dionne
September 10 @ 10:45 p.m. | Mood: Afraid

"YOU wanted my baby girl to go that bourgie-ass school, Lahron. So before your chicks, before your diamonds, before all your whips, you shoulda paid the tuition!"

Dionne winced in the darkness of her room as she stood close to her door with it opened just enough for her to peek out as her mother paced back and forth, her finger slashing through the air, and her earrings clanging like cowbells as she read her father the riot act.

"I don't need them people sending me a dang thing about Dionne's tuition, Lahron. *You* need to handle that."

Dionne closed her eyes. She had to admit this was one argument she hoped Mama won. She didn't want to leave Pace Academy. Her daddy had to pay that tuition.

"If you straight *baaallllin'*, you Jim Jones wannabe, then why these people threatening to throw Dionne out of school. Huh? Huh? Huh? Huh?"

Okay, Ma, that was a low blow, Dionne thought as she let her head rest against the door.

"What you say to me? Lahron the Don ain't nothin' but a big ole frontin' con. How you like that rap?"

Dionne actually smiled when her mama did a beat box.

"Well, I'm glad you have the money, Lahron. And your driver better have that check for my baby in the morning."

Dionne's heart soared until she felt like she had to swallow it. Yes! Yes! Yes! Dionne did a little dance in the dark, having her own little celebration party.

Beep.

"Dionne!"

She froze mid-dance.

"I know you not asleep with your little eavesdropping self. Go to bed, girl."

Still smiling, Dionne jumped across the room and landed in the center of her bed. Even though she landed with a little *whoosh* she felt like she was still floating on air.

Me See No MTV!
Posted in *uncategorized* on September 14 @ 6:00 a.m. by thedivaofdish

Just got word that Starr Lester's hopes of being on MTV's *My Super Sweet 16* were horribly dashed with yesterday's trash. Speculations ran wild after her splashy Invite Party Thursday was lacking any camera crews and bright lights.

The party is still on...but wasn't it completely more

exciting when we thought it was going to be on MTV? How embarrassing!

In other news, let's play guess who, shall we? Word on the street is the father of one of our student's latest album is a major flop. Forget platinum, this doozy didn't even hit nickel status. I definitely have my eye out for a repo alert. LOL. So...guess who.

Smooches,

Pace Academy's Diva of Dish

54 comments

thirteen

Starr
September 14 @ 6:02 a.m. | Mood: Angry. Very Angry.

The words "how embarrassing" echoed in her head like a schoolyard mocking as Starr sat at the computer with her eyes piercing the laptop screen. Up until now Starr had found the little blog amusing and made it the first thing she checked when she got up in the mornings. But now? Starr was *P-I-S-S-E-D*.

The supposed Diva of Dish had just made an enemy.

How embarrassing. How embarrassing. How embarrassing.

Starr picked up her new wireless mouse and stretched her arms high in the air. Just short of chucking it across the room, she forced herself to breathe and do the whole "Let go, let God" thing. She calmly sat the mouse back on the desk.

Being Starr wasn't easy. She would always draw attention. She would always have her fans, her stans, and her enemies. All of them were compliments to her steelo.

Still...

How embarrassing. How embarrassing. How embarrassing.

Starr had been in a horrible mood since the MTV news and she was letting her parents feel all of her funk. She did't leave her room unless she had to and she didn't speak unless spoken to. She was punishing them—that is when they were home to even notice her mini-rebellion.

But this just kicked everything up big-time.

Starr Lester didn't get played on blogs. No way.

Now she was just going to make sure that whoever the lame Diva of Dish was was going to regret not getting invited to her party. Her hater had just kicked everything up a notch and Starr was taking no prisoners.

She logged on to her Twitter account. The social networking site simply asked: What are you doing? And Starr's tweets were usually filled with fashion spotlights, random thoughts, inspirational quotes and photos of herself and any number of celebrities streaming through their home. She barely took note that she had a hundred new followers as her fingers flew across the keyboard:

STARRLESTER: I can be your best friend or your worst enemy. The choice is yours!

Starr removed her Gucci silk scarf she had tied securely around her head to keep her wrap in place. She knew she had to get ready for school but her mind was distracted.

"Knock-knock."

Swiveling her chair around, Starr faced the door. "Come in," she said, wondering who was up so early in the Lester household.

Her mother stepped into the room still dressed in a black short silk robe with her hair wrapped under a silk scarf. "You up?" she asked, rubbing the sleep from her eyes.

Starr frowned. "Yes, but why are you?" she asked in surprise. Her mother never got up before eight and even had her twin brothers trained to sleep in as well.

Sasha laughed huskily as she walked over to lean against Starr's desk. "Your father had to leave for an early video shoot and you know he woke me up."

"Where did he go?" Starr asked, rising from her seat to stretch her limbs in her Juicy Couture romper.

"He's in the city." Sasha stretched and yawned as she looked around Starr's room. "I wish I had a room like this when I was growing up."

Starr shrugged as she walked over to her closet for one of the dreaded uniforms.

"Something wrong, Starr?"

She turned to eye her mother, wondering if this was a chance for one of their rare mother-daughter talks. "Some of the kids at school were clowning that my party won't be on MTV," Starr said. She was actually surprised at herself. For one, that she told her mom. And also that Diva of Dish had gotten to her.

Sasha waved her hand dismissively. "Haters throw

shade because they hate to see someone shine," she said. "Don't worry about a bunch of silly school kids, Starr."

Starr opened her mouth. She wanted to say, *I'm one of those school kids.*

"But Ma, people are laughing at me."

"What should I do?" Sasha rose to her feet. "We'll go shopping when you get home from school," she said, turning to leave Starr's bedroom. "Retail therapy cures everything."

Starr eyed her computer. "Actually, I saw a few things I wanted online," she began. "Can I just order those?"

"Go 'head," she said over her shoulder with another yawn before closing the bedroom door behind her.

Starr tossed her uniform toward the end of her bed as she eased back over to her desk. One by one she logged into her Barney, Nordstrom, Neiman and Bergdorf accounts and used her father's credit card info to pay for the items she had saved in her shopping cart.

A pair of Chloé boots here.

A Stella McCartney outfit there.

New undies. An organic romper. A new gold clutch.

The total came to somewhere around two grand. A little light shopping that did absolutely nothing to make Starr feel better.

Having a party to top all parties *and* the Diva of Dumbass's head on a platter would have to do that.

fourteen

Marisol
September 14 @ 10:45 a.m. | Mood: Amorous

TOday was the last day of taping for the documentary about her father, and just like every other time the swarm of cameras and crew was at her house, she was dressed to the nines. The BCBG sleeveless bib dress she wore was so very completely different from her usual Sunday attire of leggings and a fitted tee. She loved the way the charcoal looked against her bronze complexion. She put on very light makeup, and with one last shake of her now-curly black locks, Marisol slipped her feet into a pair of suede gladiators and slid her BlackBerry into the hidden pocket of her dress before she left her room.

Marisol had discovered that she loved the cameras and they were crushing on her, as well. And she used the opportunity well, being sure to be wherever the cameras were when her dad was filming. Her impromptu fashion show this week served two purposes. She was well aware that her image was going to be in millions of homes and...

"*Hola*, Corey," Marisol said in her best flirty voice as she walked into the large and airy—and thankfully empty—kitchen. *Remember, Marisol. Smile. Just enough to say "I like you" but not enough to scream "I'm psycho."*

He stopped wrapping a thick black cord around his arm to look over at her with a quick smile. "Hi, Marisol," he said, before he stooped down to place the cord in a large black case. "You look pretty as always."

Marisol's heart soared. She knew it was today or never. She was *soooo* tired of waiting for him to make the first move. How many times had she tried to will him, through mind control, to ask her out? She really wasn't going to accept the premise of the book *He's Just Not That Into You.*

"We're wrapping up here after your parents do the tour of the house," he began, looking at her with eyes that made her heart race like she just finished a mad dash through a Neiman's sale.

Marisol pouted to let him know how much of a downer his leaving was.

"Maybe we could hang out sometime," Corey offered, leaning back against the edge of the floor-to-ceiling cabinets.

Yippeee! In the privacy of her room she would do a

flip. Marisol reached out and lightly touched his hand. "Not maybe. *Definitely.*"

They both whipped out their cell phones and programmed each other's numbers, e-mail and social networking sites. It was always necessary for couples to stay in touch.

Corey's eyes fell on Marisol's glossy lips as he slid his cell phone back in the pocket of his jeans.

He's gonna kiss me. Yes! Just wait until I tell Starr and Dionne. Marisol wished she had time to do a breath check. As he lowered his head toward her, she closed her eyes and raised her chin the way she saw the women do on *Days of Our Lives.*

"Corey!"

He jumped back from her and bumped his head on the cabinet.

And that irked Marisol big-time, but she held her fiery temper in check. He rubbed the back of his head as he strode toward the bellowing voice in the living room. She stomped her foot in frustration.

"Something wrong, Marisol?" her mother asked in Spanish from behind her suddenly.

Marisol turned and smiled at how beautiful her *madre* looked in a burnt-orange jumpsuit with chunky turquoise accessories. Picture-perfect and ready for her close-up. Like mother, like daughter.

People said Yasmine Rivera resembled a taller, fuller version of the Latina beauty Eva Longoria. Marisol had once overheard her mother joke with her friends that she was more of a desperate housewife than Eva's television character.

Marisol just shook her head with a small smile.

"All these people in our home. I am so happy this is the last day," Yasmine said as she retrieved some bottled water from the stainless-steel Viking fridge.

"Not me, Mami, we're going to be on television," Marisol said excitedly. *And I'm going to have a boyfriend!*

Yasmine watched her daughter as she took a sip from the bottled water. "You are growing up so fast, Marisol," she said in Spanish, as she screwed the cap back on the bottle. "I remember when you were just a baby in my arms."

Marisol leaned against the massive granite-topped island in the center of the kitchen. "*That* was a long time ago," she stressed, desperately wanting to be seen as a young woman and not a little girl.

Yasmine moved around the island and playfully bumped her hip against her daughter's. "Protect your heart and your innocence. Don't be in a rush to give them away," she advised. "Life is always filled with regrets."

Marisol looked up at her mom and the sadness in her beautiful brown eyes was clear. Seriously.

At that moment, Marisol's dad strolled into the kitchen with his camera crew right on his heels.

"Yasmine, they're ready for us to tour the house," Alexandro said as he walked up to her and placed a kiss on her forehead.

Yasmine's smile was in place as soon as the lights and the camera shone in her eyes but Marisol didn't miss the way her mom moved away from her father by walking back to the fridge to grab a bottle of water. She hadn't even finished drinking the one already sitting on the island.

Marisol looked around at the crew and noticed Corey was absent. *Maybe we can find a quiet spot for that kiss,* she thought as she eased past the camera crew out of the kitchen. She dug her peach-flavored lip gloss out of her pocket and glazed her mouth really well as she searched for her new boyfriend. *Yes!*

She found him in the foyer and smiled as she walked up behind him quietly.

"I miss you, too, baby girl. But my dad wants me to work with him."

Marisol stopped. Her eyes widened a bit right along with her mouth as her heart hammered like *crazy.*

"Ask your mom if I can take you to the movies tonight," Corey said.

Oh…heck…no! This clown already has a girl!

Marisol leaned against the wall, crossed her arms over her chest and waited patiently.

"A'ight, I'll see you later."

Corey turned and his eyes got big—saucer big—as he faced Marisol.

Suddenly Corey, "the Cheater," wasn't looking so yummy anymore.

"One thing you don't know about me, Corey, is I don't

do secondhand," Marisol said as she stepped forward and plucked his cell phone that had been still in his hand. "Erase me from your contacts."

As she turned and walked away, Marisol's mother's words of advice came floating back to her in a whisper:

"Protect your heart and your innocence. Don't be in a rush to give them away. Life is always filled with regrets."

True.

fifteen

Dionne
September 14 @ 11:45 a.m. | Mood: Confused

DIONNE *hated* Sundays with a passion.

Sundays meant another weekend of fabulousness was over.

She snuggled deeper under the covers of her four-poster bed in her bedroom at her daddy's posh duplex apartment. The last thing she wanted to do was face the start of this day, but her stomach was growling like crazy and she was ready to see her daddy. He wasn't home when she got in from Starr's yesterday afternoon. She'd thought she heard him come in late last night, but she hadn't bothered to get up and check...especially since the last time she went running in her dad's room she saw way more of him and his latest girlfriend than she *ever* cared to see.

Her new Keyshia Cole ringtone filled the quiet of her

room. Dionne sat up straight in the middle of the bed causing the colorful pillows to fly over the edge onto the floor.

She flipped the Sidekick open.

Hassan.

Dionne knew she couldn't avoid him forever and truthfully she didn't really want to. She really liked Hassan's swagger. She really liked Hassan. Period.

Still she sent his call straight to voice mail.

Hassan didn't fit into her world anymore. For now memories of their flirting game was all she had left to hold on to.

Dionne rolled out of bed and made her way into her bathroom to squash any morning breath, leaving any thoughts of Hassan and his serious swagger behind *with* the phone. Once she made sure she was minty fresh and not funky fresh, Dionne left her bedroom and walked down to the end of the hall to the master suite.

Knowing her daddy had a late night she hated to wake him so early, but if he was home they *always* had Sunday-morning breakfast together before her driver took her home to Newark.

"Rise and shine, Pops," Dionne called through the solid mahogany door that was as black as hair dye. She knocked two times.

Female giggles mixed with her daddy's deep laughter filtered through the door. *Hoochie in the house.* Dionne rolled her eyes heavenward before she crossed her thin arms over her chest, pouting with major attitude on her face.

Seconds later the black door opened and the thick haze of marijuana smoke escaped the room and surrounded her head like her own personal rain cloud. Dionne fanned it away with her hand, her bracelets clinking as she did. Her daddy and his whole crew loved the sticky-icky.

She stepped inside the room, instantly ignoring the blond-haired, dark-skinned, big-butt woman walking her bare-naked, cottage-cheese dimpled behind into the bathroom. *Eew!*

And there lying in the middle of his bed in all his splendor is platinum-selling rap artist, used-to-be TRL mainstay (before it went off the air), hip-hop magazine cover model, *106 & Park* video count champ Lahron the Don. And all of the accoutrements of his hip-hop swagger were already in place—platinum and diamond chains, sagging True Religion jeans, fresh fade and a mouthful of grills. Downstairs were two expensive rides waiting in his spots in the underground garage. His fancy apartment was a long way from his days growing up in the Bricks.

"Really, Daddy, you need to open a window, big-time," Dionne complained as she eyed him flipping through channels on his flat-screen television on the opposite wall.

"For what?" he asked, pretending to be innocent with a big, bleach-whitened toothy grin.

Dionne arched an eyebrow as she wove her fingers through the disarray of her hair. "Puh-*leeze*, Daddy," she drawled, way past the days of faking like she didn't know the smell of weed.

Lahron stood up and stretched his slender six-foot-five frame before using one hand to yank up his sagging jeans. "You better not let me catch you smokin', ya heard me?" he ordered more than asked in that gravelly voice his fans loved.

"Weed leads to other drugs. And I've lived around enough fiends and 'heads to know I'm not gone be one, Daddy," she told him truthfully, wondering when he got the newest tattoo of her baby picture on his shoulder. It added to the dozen other tats all over his frame.

Yet, she couldn't get a tiny, itsy-bitsy rose tattoo on her wrist. Yet another example of his "do as I say and not as I do" parenting. *Bet Starr could get a tattoo if she wanted to,* Dionne thought even though Starr was deathly afraid of needles so there was no chance of her even asking. Plus they were too young for any legit tat artist, but in the hood *anything* was possible...

"What's for breakfast?" Dionne asked, ignoring the *huge* black-and-white sketch of the naked and squatting woman over his bed as she looked around his room.

Lahron walked over to his ebony wood nightstand and grabbed a wad of cash. "Order something in, go wash, and let me handle June Bug," he told her, reaching out to affectionately tweak her nose as he did.

Handle meant send her on her way.

Deuces, Dionne thought. That was more than fine with her as she reached up to kiss his cheek before she left the room.

It was daddy-daughter time. Period.

* * *

The ride from New York to Newark didn't really reveal that much difference. Just more tall buildings, more people walking the streets and more cars making traffic crazy. Still, Dionne felt the change as she sat in the rear of the car headed back to reality.

She wished her daddy could have driven her himself. But instead Mindy, his personal assistant, who was white and seemed more like a librarian than part of a rapper's entourage, drove her home looking like she thought they were about to get carjacked at any moment.

As Mindy's little yellow Volkswagen Bug made a right onto Sixteenth Avenue, Dionne looked out at Westside Park. There was a baseball game being played and the bleachers were packed with onlookers. *Humph,* she thought. *They make it seem like people in the hood only robbed and got high, or ran from people who robbed and got high. Stereotypes. Whateva.*

Dionne thought about her own lies to her friends about where she lived, but she pushed any feelings of guilt away. It wasn't the same. It just wasn't.

Mindy had brought her home plenty of times so she knew exactly where she was going and you would think by now she would ease up and realize the whole city of Newark wasn't waiting around a corner to rob her. As the car neared the three-family apartment building where Dionne lived, she noticed her friends Joshia and Kim walking up the street from the corner store with chips and sodas in their hands.

Dionne smiled at the sight of them as she lowered the window. She stuck her head out as she ignored Mindy glancing over at her like she was worried the boogeyman was about to jump through the window. "Hey, divas!" she hollered, reaching behind her to wave her hand for Mindy to slow the car down. Mindy didn't.

Joshia and Kim both looked over at her and then made a point of looking away. Dionne's face fell. She had been dissed and dismissed. She knew she didn't spend as much time with her girls since she started at Pace, but was it really all of that? She frowned as she sat back in the passenger seat, cutting her eyes to watch them in the rearview mirror. They were laughing and having fun. *Without me,* she thought as Mindy's car pulled to a stop.

As she gathered her Gucci duffel and pocketbook and climbed out of the car, Dionne looked up and noticed Hassan sitting on her stoop with his earphones on listening to his iPod. Her heart beat faster as she turned and bent down to look inside the car. "Thanks, Mindy."

Mindy's eyes shifted from Hassan to Dionne. "He's totally hot," she said, with an overly dramatic wink.

Dionne's face became pained. She had to make herself not frown. There was nothing worse than an adult trying so hard to be cool. "All right. Bye," she said with emphasis, stepping back to firmly close the door and send Mindy on her way.

As she stepped up to the brick step, Dionne let herself enjoy the sight that was Hassan Ali. Tall, dark as chocolate, fade shining and freshly cut, cubic zirconia bling shining from his ear and a brightly colored hoodie that perfectly matched his Nikes. There wasn't a boy at Pace who could touch Hassan.

"What's up, stranger?" he asked as he jogged down the stairs to pull her close for a hug.

"Nothing much, what's up with you?" Dionne asked as she stepped back out of his embrace.

Hassan leaned back and looked at her before he shrugged and slid his hands in the front pockets of his jeans. "Just thought I'd come and check on you since—"

Just then Dionne's Sidekick began to vibrate on her hip. His eyes dropped down to it. "So your phone do work."

Dionne licked her glossy lips. "Hassan, I—"

"Uhm, uhm, uhm. How *you* doin', Hassan?"

Dionne looked over her shoulder at Joshia and Kim walking up to them. Joshia ignored Dionne as she reached up to stroke his square cheek. "Still fine as always," she said in a soft and flirtatious voice.

Dionne went from being hurt that they were ignoring her, like Starr ignored out-of-season clothes, to being mad. Unlike Marisol and Starr, they knew she liked Hassan. So one of them stepping to Hassan in such a bold way was like a dare for her to say something. Dionne wasn't even going to get punked by nobody. "And he's busy, so bounce," Dionne snapped, ready to swing out at one or both of them if necessary.

Joshia was short, thick and curvy but she knew Dionne could and would spank that butt if necessary. Still she turned and stepped in Dionne's face anyway.

Dionne dropped her book bag.

Hassan held up his hands and jumped in between them. "Dang, man, ain't y'all friends?" he asked in surprise.

"Humph," Joshia said with plenty of attitude as she eyed Dionne from head to toe with attitude. "Forget that bourgie chick."

"Forget that jealous chick," Dionne threw back at her over Hassan's broad shoulder.

"Jealous?" Both Joshia and Kim screeched as if in shock.

"Don't hate...CON-GRA-TU-LATE," Dionne screeched back.

Hassan bent down to snatch up her book bag before he guided her up the stairs of the porch by her shoulders. "Come on, Didi," he urged.

Dionne glared at her old friends/new enemies over her shoulder until she walked into the dimly lit entry hall of the building. "I can't believe them," she said, crossing her arms over her chest as she paced in front of the mailboxes in the wall.

Hassan handed over her book bag and shook his head sadly. "I can't believe you either," he told her.

Dionne paused and turned to look up at him. "Huh?"

Hassan reached out and stroked her cheek, before he turned and opened the door. "I'm not callin' you no more, Dionne. And if you take too long to call me I'm not gonna answer."

With that he walked out the door leaving Dionne feeling big-time crushed.

sixteen

Starr
September 19 @ 10:45 a.m. | Mood: Pissed! ☹

starr paced the length of the sitting room of the bathroom as she waited for her friends. They needed each other now more than ever.

Until now she had been having a good day—a great day, in fact. First, she woke up to the news that her dad had hired her her very own production crew to capture every moment of her party planning and the ultimate party night. Second, the tastings for her Sylvia Weinstock cake were divine. She couldn't wait for the moment when the cake would rise up from the floor of the stage for all to stare in awe and envy. And last, all of the students who had not been invited to her birthday bash were falling at her feet begging for an invite. Of course, they could forget about it. Her guest list was set, but she loved all the extra attention anyway. And best of all?

Starr whipped out her cell phone and scrolled through her incoming texts.

JORDAN: NEED 2 TALK 2 U. CAN U MEET ME AT THE GYM DURING LUNCH?
UR#1STARR: K.

Starr had been floating on clouds one through nine since she'd gotten Jordan's text. But all her joy faded when someone showed her the latest post on the Diva of Dish's blog.

The door opened and Marisol walked in with her cell phone still in her hand, her brown face flushed.

"What's the emergency? I was in my music class across campus."

"Wait on Dionne," Starr told her, as she continued to pace.

Seconds later the door opened and Dionne walked in. Her long straight hair was in a ponytail and she was still dressed in gym clothes. "What's the emergency?" she asked, parroting Marisol.

"Outside of my party, we have one goal and one goal only, ladies," Starr told them, turning on the heels of her new Fendi pumps.

Dionne and Marisol shared a long look before turning curious eyes back to their friend and leader, or was it leader and friend?

"The Diva of Dumb just posted ten reasons why everyone at Pace should hate the Pacesetters."

"Ooh," the girls said in unison with angry scowls on their faces.

Starr continued pacing. "It's probably one of those losers, who didn't get an invite to the party," she pondered aloud as if plotting battle strategies. "But!"

Dionne and Marisol jumped back as Starr whirled around on them like a tornado.

"If I find out that someone I have invited to my Fierce and Fabulous Fashionista Fifteen party—"

"I thought it was just Fashionista Fifteen?" Marisol said, her Spanish accent more pronounced.

Dionne nodded. "Yeah, me, too. When did you change it, Starr?" she asked, turning to look up at her.

Starr clenched her fists and released a high-pitched scream at the top of her lungs. "WHO GIVES A FLIP ABOUT THAT RIGHT NOW?" she roared.

"Wooooooooooooow," Dionne and Marisol said, leaning away from her.

Starr immediately pulled herself together as she smoothed her hands over the stiff pleats of her uniform skirt. "Ladies, let's just find out who's the Diva of Dish."

Starr stuck her hand out, her short manicured nails covered with Bad Girl Black.

Marisol placed her hand on top of Starr's, her Back-to-the-'80s neon-green nails glowing brightly.

And then Dionne covered Marisol's hand with her new pink-and-white French manicure.

"One…two…three…PACESETTERS!"

* * *

Starr didn't tell her girls about her "meeting" with Jordan. If things turned out well—like Jordan dropping to one knee to shout out his love for her—then she would consider it. But for now—good or bad—it was her little secret. Plus, it didn't matter because she had a dozen more.

She barely took in the well-manicured landscape of the campus as she made her way toward the sports complex. She had barely made her way through the automated revolving doors when she spotted Jordan sitting on the metal steps leading to the second floor. His head was down and she could tell he was lost in the music playing through the earphones of his iPod.

She paused when he lifted his head and sang:

"*Don't know how to tell you that I love ya...Can't find the words to even explain...Whenever I'm near you I just want to touch ya...you're the type of girl to make me lose my game.*'"

Starr completely lost her breath. It wasn't just the words, but Jordan's voice. It was Jordan's vocal arrangement. His emotions showed so clearly on his face. He was just simply being Jordan.

He opened his eyes and smiled sheepishly to find her standing there.

Starr took a breath to compose herself before her crush on him was written all over her face, not just deep in her heart. She clapped as she strolled over to him. "How much do I owe you for the front-row seat to the concert?" she asked him, remembering all the rules of covert flirting.

Soft eyes. Soft smile. Softly spoken words. Starr had it down pat.

"I'd sing for you anytime, Starr. Just ask," he told her with a smile as he rose to his full height and walked down the stairs to come and stand before her. Somehow he made that stupid red blazer and stiff gray slacks look like Gucci.

Speak, Starr. Speak!

She just laughed kind of nervously, completely hating that she sounded like a big-time cornball.

Jordan reached out to lightly touch her hand. "Hey, I'm sorry about that stupid blog."

Starr was amazed that standing there in front of Jordan, feeling his touch, smelling his cologne, she could care less about the blog or the Dumb Diva—at least for now anyway.

"Is that what you wanted to talk to me about?" she asked him softly.

Jordan glanced away for just a second. He opened his mouth to say something and then closed it. He glanced away again...for another second. "I wanted...I just wanted to make sure you were okay."

Starr didn't completely believe him, but she let it be because, she wasn't quite ready to reveal her cards either.

So the flirting dance continued.

seventeen

Dionne
September 21 @ 11:45 a.m. | Mood: Afraid...Again

"YO, Dionne, come here!"

She looked up from the teen magazine she was flipping through before she rolled off her bed. She padded barefoot to her father's office, standing in the doorway. "Whaddup, Daddy?" she asked, eyeing him sitting behind a huge black desk with his laptop in front of him.

"Come look at what somebody sent me?"

Dionne walked across the spacious room and around the desk to look down at the computer screen. She frowned a little and then smiled. "Ooh, I look cute," she said, eyeing the black-and-white photo of her posing with her father. "That's going in *Essence,* right?"

"Damn right," Lahron the Don said, leaning back in the chair to look up at her.

The celebrity magazine had a feature spread with up-and-coming hip-hop artists and their families. It had been fun modeling, getting makeup done and being dressed by a stylist—but Dionne had especially enjoyed sharing her father's celebrity world with him. She was excited to see all the photos.

His cell phone on top of his desk vibrated and Lahron grabbed it up. "Yo, whaddup?"

As soon as her father hopped out of his seat and walked out of the office, Dionne dropped into it to open each and every photo file.

"Oooh, cute," she whispered as she eyed her casual but fab style in the photo. Her hair, her natural-looking makeup and her outfit were all on point.

She was deciding whether to forward the picture to her own e-mail address when she caught sight of an open letter on top of the desk. Her frown deepened as she glimpsed the words: *DELINQUENT, URGENT, LEGAL.*

Glancing out the door to be sure her father wasn't coming back, Dionne turned the letter so that she could read it. And she didn't like what she read one bit.

Her father's stylist was requesting payment in full for nearly five thousand dollars for services rendered. First her school tuition and now this. Dionne picked up the letter and underneath it lay several more letters along the same lines of the first letter.

"What the…"

She thought of the check her father used to pay her

tuition in full. *Oh, good grief, is it gonna bounce?* she thought. Em-barr-a-ssing!!

She set the letter back down, the photos forgotten as she leaned back in the leather chair.

Lahron walked back into the office and Dionne cut her eyes over at the three diamond chains dangling around his neck. "Daddy, is everything okay?" she asked, her stomach in knots.

He glanced at her before picking up his glass of soda from the edge of the desk. "What you talking about?"

"Money wise. Is everything okay—because you don't have to buy me all those clothes, especially since I wear uniforms to school."

Lahron's eyes shifted to the letters on his desk. He came around the front of the desk to lean against it as he looked down at her. "First off, I didn't call you in here to read something that doesn't belong to you. Secondly, I'm not broke—I'm just bad at paying bills on time."

Dionne's eyes were immediately apologetic. "I'm sorry, Daddy, I shouldn't have been snooping," she told him.

"That's cool, but remember I ain't broke at all," he continued to protest...perhaps a bit too much.

Dionne leaned forward in the chair to continue clicking through the pictures. "Got it," she said, wishing she had never brought it up.

Lahron reached in the pockets of his vintage faded jeans and pulled out wads of money. Dionne's eyes shifted to take in the crisp bills. "I got it, Dad," Dionne drawled again.

Lahron tapped his chest and held his arms outstretched. "Do you see where your daddy is living and what whips I'm driving?"

Dionne turned in the chair, leaned back and crossed her arms over her chest. "Daddy. Seriously. I just asked a question. I got it. You're not broke."

"If I was broke would I offer to buy you and your mama a house?" he stressed.

Dionne sat up straight in the chair. "Our own house?" she asked excitedly.

At his nod, she bounced from the chair and flung herself into her father's arms. "Thank you, Daddy."

"No, don't thank me yet because you know your mama don't want nothing from me."

Dionne leaned back to look up at him. "She said no?"

Lahron moved past Dionne to reclaim his seat at the desk. "You know that."

Dionne smiled as she allowed herself to dream. She thought of all the fabulous things that would be hers with their own house: a bigger room, a better neighborhood, no more lying to Starr and Marisol, she could even finally have sleepovers.

"Dionne."

Ooh, maybe even a house with a pool and a big backyard! FAB-U-LOUS!

"Dionne."

She cut her eyes over at her father as her imaginings came to an abrupt end.

"Are we straight about this money thing?" he asked as he reached for his drink again.

"Yeah, uh-huh," she said almost dismissively as she turned and walked out of the room with a million plans as to how to talk her mama into accepting the house.

eighteen

Starr
September 21 @ 7:08 p.m. | Mood: Studious

STARR was sitting on the cushioned window seat reading her history textbook for an upcoming quiz when the doorbell to her suite rang. She frowned as she picked up the oversize remote pad and switched on her plasma television to the channel linked to the surveillance camera outside her door.

She assumed it wasn't her parents, since they knew the combination for the electronic keypad. And she hadn't asked Mimi to bring her anything, so she was beyond curious about who was interrupting her study time.

"Who in the...hello and goodbye...is *she?*" Starr said with an attitude as she eyed the tall white teenage girl with a riot of bright red curls standing outside the door to her suite, looking totally bored.

Barefoot and in leggings and a fitted tee, Starr walked

across the plush carpet to get a closer look at the girl on her plasma TV. She worked the control pad to make the surveillance camera slowly angle up and then down to take in everything about the stranger standing at her door.

Her eyebrows arched as she quickly took in the girl's trendy laid-back style in her skinny jeans, high-heeled booties and fitted tee with several gold chains around her neck, which gave her look more polish and edge. Starr knew just by looking at her that her style was effortless, just like her beauty.

Who is she?

Starr set down the remote control console on the edge of her bed. Her doorbell chimed again as she scooped up her cordless and dialed her parents' private line.

"Hey, Starr," her mother said, the sound of laughter and chatter in the background. "Are you and Natalie getting along?"

Starr rolled her eyes heavenward. "No, because Natalie is standing outside my door working my doorbell *and* my nerves," she snapped. "Who is she?"

"Excuse me for a second?" she heard her mother say to her guests.

Starr tapped her foot and turned to watch the girl still standing at her door.

"Starr Lester, you open up that door and let her in," Sasha said in a scolding whisper that really wasn't a whisper at all.

"Mama," Starr protested.

"Her parents are good friends of mine and I know she doesn't want to hang around with us."

"Ma-aaah," Starr whined.

"You should invite her to the party," Sasha suggested.

Starr pulled the phone away to stare at it as if her mother had lost her mind. "No invites. I don't even know this girl—why should she experience all the fabulousness of *my* party?"

Sasha sighed.

"All right, I'm letting her in."

"That's my Starr."

She made a face as she hung up the phone and flung it onto the center of her bed. "Coming," she called out, already bounding across the room and through the open doors of her closet. She quickly undressed and started changing her clothes.

In no time she was dressed in an ivory Nanette Lepore tunic, gold gladiator sandals and had even touched up her lip gloss. There was no way Starr Lester was letting anyone outdress her in her own house. Oh, no. That was a big-time no.

Starr pulled open the door and had to tilt her head back to look up at the Amazon.

With a nonchalant expression she looked past Starr as she openly scrutinized the suite. "Whaddup, I'm Natalie. Your mom said I could come up and chill with you."

Starr's mouth fell open. This girl looked paler than someone from Utah. But when she opened her mouth, she sounded like Alicia Keys—husky and throaty, like she was black! *What the hello and goodbye?*

"Uhhhm, come in," Starr said, stepping back to wave her into her suite.

"Nice room," she said, walking around.

"I have my own screening room, spa bath and room-size walk-in closet," Starr boasted.

Natalie nodded. "Your suite is almost as big as mine," she said, sitting down on one of the four club chairs situated around a round, low-slung table. She picked up one of Starr's many fashion magazines and flipped through it like she was bored.

Starr couldn't stand her. Period. Point-blank. Ready-forhertogo.com. Carryyourselfouttahere.net.

"So you don't go to Pace, do you?" Starr asked, licking her lips as she sat in one of the club chairs. She made sure to cross her legs and maintain an elegant pose.

Natalie made a face. "I wish. I go to Knightsbridge Day School," she said as she flicked the pages of the magazine resting in her lap.

Knightsbridge was even more prestigious than Pace. Most of the students were children of wealthy families whose fortunes dated back generations.

"I bet Pace is way more fun," she said, glancing over at Starr with emerald-green eyes.

Starr shook her head. "No, not really. Pace is kind of lame actually," she lied.

Natalie just shrugged and continued to flip through the magazine.

As Starr peeped at Natalie's style, she thought to herself that she never wanted Natalie to come to Pace Academy—ever.

She was thin, pretty, stylish and self-assured—a white version of herself. And she definitely wasn't interested in having any competition.

No, Natalie needed to stay at Knightsbridge and on her side of town, because there was room for only one queen bee at Pace Academy and it most definitely was Starr Lester. Period. The end.

Starr couldn't wait for her parents' guests to leave, since she was more than ready to see Natalie go. Bye, girl!

nineteen

Marisol
September 21 @ 7:45 p.m. | Mood: Excited

Marisol hated to hurry through her bath in her clawfoot tub. Especially since her favorite bath supplies from Fresh had arrived. She absolutely loved their skincare line's use of natural ingredients like milk, soy and rice. The clear jars of various scents and products were neatly stacked inside the armoire in the corner of her ultra bathroom. With one last leisurely stretch in sweet-smelling, soothing water, Marisol released the drain, allowing the last remnants of body polish to disappear. It was worth every bit of the hefty price tag.

She allowed herself just a few precious moments of moisturizing her skin before she wrapped a plush towel around her body and hurried out of her adjoining bathroom into her bedroom. There was a hard knock to her door.

"¡Marisol, la mamá dijó se apresura!"

Marisol rolled her eyes at the sound of her brother's yelling for her to hurry up through the door. *He's probably putting boogers on my doorknob,* she thought as she pulled her hair into a loose and messy topknot. She snatched on a lime-green tube top maxi dress before grabbing her cell phone as she rushed from the room.

Tonight both her mother and her father's family were coming over to watch a rough-cut preview of the documentary about her father. Although the whole thing was a reminder of her broken hopes with Cheater Corey, Marisol was excited to see herself on the big screen and spend time with her family. She did not have time for wannabe playas. *Puh-leeze.*

El lo podría mantener moviendo con eso. (He could keep it moving with that.)

She just was disappointed that her girls couldn't be there. Starr was busy with her mom and her party planner. And Didi went with her dad to some Nickelodeon event in L.A. for the weekend.

Marisol's stomach growled at the scent of the food being prepared by the staff in the kitchen as she continued past it on her way to the media room. Even though she was keeping her eyes on her Latin-flavored hips, Marisol had every intention of chowing down and then working up a sweat exercising away the extra calories.

Ding.

Marisol paused at the double doors leading into the media room and checked her phone for the incoming text.

UR#1STARR: LOOK AT THE SHOES I FOUND 4 MY OUTFIT. OW!!!

Marisol hurried to open the photo. Starr and her mom were both smiling as they held up a pair of Gucci high-heel ankle-strap platform sandals in gold. They were wicked. The heels were so high that Marisol was surprised that even a laid-back mom like Sasha was letting Starr wear them.

MARIMARI: LUV THEM. LUV THEM. LUV THEM.
DIVADIDI: U R SOOO LUCKY. MY MOM WOULD KILL ME.
MARIMARI: MINE 2. ☹
UR#1STARR: REMEMBER THE DRESS CODE IS ALL WHITE.
DIVADIDI: STILL HAVE TO FIND SUM'N 2 WEAR.
MARIMARI: ME 2. ☺
UR#1STARR: REALLY MISS U GUYS.

"Marisol!"

MARIMARI: MISS U 2. GOTTA GO.
DIVADIDI: DEUCES LADIES.
UR#1STARR: SMOOCHES.

Marisol walked into the spacious media room, which was filled to capacity—it was standing room only. Marisol made her way to the front of the stylishly appointed room and sat on the floor in between her mother and father's feet.

"Remember, Marisol, time is money," Alex told her before he playfully tugged at her topknot.

"Yes, sir."

The lights dimmed and the curtain covering the wall

opened wide. Marisol knew her *padre* was working one of his touch-screen remote control systems designed to run the entire house.

Marisol and the entire family laughed and talked throughout the entire screening, which was clearly a rough cut and still needed editing. Anytime she was on the huge screen Marisol blew herself kisses, loving that she looked big-time fabulous in every single shot…just like her mother.

Midway through the viewing, Marisol jumped to her feet as she felt something wet drizzle on her head and down her back. She whirled and the look of pain and shock on her mother's face surprised her. "Mama, what's wrong?" Marisol asked.

Her eyes darted to her father. His entire body was stiff and he dropped his head down into his hand. The entire family became quiet as all eyes locked on her parents and not the screen.

"I'm sorry, everyone. The glass must have slipped from my hand," Yasmine said, rising to hand Marisol napkins without looking her or anyone else in the eyes.

"Will you all excuse me?" Yasmine said politely with a soft smile.

Marisol looked on in confusion as her mother pushed past their family members and guests and left the screening room.

"Everyone please finish watching the show and I'll go check on Yasmine," her father said, rising to his feet. "Maybe she's not feeling well."

One of Marisol's *tías* helped blot the water from her

shoulders and back before she dropped down into her mother's leather theater chair. The laughter continued and her parents' disappearance was forgotten…by everyone but Marisol.

Where are they?

Is Mamá sick?

What's going on?

Marisol knew that whatever it was it had to be major because her parents were the ultimate hosts and they would never leave guests alone like this.

Marisol barely took her eyes off the screen as it filled with her image as she walked into the kitchen. She knew the moment oh, so very well. It was right after she caught Corey on the phone with his girlfriend.

Her heart tugged a little at the look of sadness in her eyes and the fake smile on her lips. Big-time truth? That little weeklong crush had really hurt. It was her first experience with a guy cheating.

"Marisol, look," her little brother Carlos said before he came around to plop down in their father's theater chair.

She looked down at him and all of his black curly hair and brown skin. He really was cute.

Carlos pulled a booger from his nose, rolled it and then plucked it clear across the room.

Too bad he was so gross.

Ugh!

Marisol ignored him for the rest of the screening, her

eyes constantly darting to the door, awaiting her parents' return. But her hopes kept getting dashed.

Marisol used the massive remote control to turn up the lights after the screen faded to black. She rose to her feet. "Excuse me, everyone. Please go into the dining room for all that good food," she told them, slipping right into the role of hostess in her mom's absence. Yasmine had taught her well.

She whirled around just in time to see Carlos about to touch her. "Keep your hands off, my booger boy," she snapped, with her brown eyes flashing as she pointed her finger against his forehead. "And go wash your hands. Now!"

Marisol eased through the crowd of people filing out of the media room, her bare feet lightly tapping against the floors as she quickly made her way down the long hallway to race up the steps. Her heart was pounding as she crept nearer to her parents' bedroom and pressed her ear to the wood.

They were arguing—in Spanish. It couldn't be good.

"Stay away from me, Alex. I hate you. I hate you."

Marisol's eyes widened as she nervously bit her nail, leaving tiny chips of Pleasure Principle Purple nail polish on the tip of her tongue.

"Yasmine, let me explain."

"Explain what? Huh? Explain what, Alex? Explain why *that* woman was at the baseball field. Explain that."

Slap.

Marisol gasped at the sound of what she knew was her

mother's hand connecting with her father's face. Woman? Baseball field? What?

"All of these women only want you for your name and your money. You think if you had nothing all those women would throw themselves at you. You risk your family for that, Alex? I loved you when you had nothing."

Marisol rose to her feet and tore away from her parents' door and their private business. She had no right to eavesdrop. She heard way more than any fifteen-year-old ever wanted—or needed—to know.

The world as she knew it suddenly felt different.

A crazy dream. Nightmare. Bad sitcom script.

Marisol rushed through the house and made her way back to the now-empty media room. With trembling fingers she used the remote to rewind the DVD back to the point where her mother had dropped her drink on her.

Her eyes flittered across the screen as she chewed off more Pleasure Principle Purple, looking for something that only her mother had seen and recognized. She jumped and jabbed the pause button with her finger.

Paused on the hundred-inch screen, just barely in the frame, Marisol's clear eyes locked on the blond-haired woman climbing into a flashy red Porsche. The woman's moment on the screen had been so quick, but it had been enough for her mother to see.

And unfortunately it was enough for Marisol.

How can I ever look at my father the same?

She dropped into one of the theater chairs, pulling her feet up to her knees before she pulled her maxi dress down over them.

Are my parents getting divorced? she thought.

Marisol thought of how she felt when she found out that her crush had a girlfriend and she hated that her mother had to feel that at all.

"Protect your heart and your innocence. Don't be in a rush to give them away. Life is always filled with regrets."

She turned as the media-room door opened. Carlos stuck his curly head in. "Marisol, Mama said to come and eat. Everyone is waiting for you."

Marisol just nodded but she didn't move. She couldn't.

Carlos walked over to her. "Something wrong, Mari?" he asked, his cute face filled with concern.

Something was big-time wrong.

"No, Carlos," she lied, reaching up to muss his hair with a smile, a very sad smile.

twenty

Starr
September 22 @ 6:30 a.m. | Mood: Disappointed

STARR was headed out the door when she remembered the parent-teacher conference was today. She dropped her Vuitton book bag and turned to head back up the stairs to her parents' bedroom suite. She knocked twice on the towering double doors.

Yes, it was early.

Yes, she knew they were asleep.

No, she didn't care.

"Come in," her mom called out groggily.

Starr opened one of the doors and peeked her head inside. The room was pitch-dark and she could barely make out their massive bed in the center of the room. "Ma, don't forget the parent-teacher conference today," she said, squinting her eyes.

"We won't," was the groggy reply.

Starr persisted. "Please don't forget. They're starting to think I raise myself," she said.

"Starr, we'll be there," her father added.

Starr knew she was pushing it when her father stepped in, but she didn't care. "Your word is supposed to be your bond."

"Starr!" they both exclaimed.

She could barely make out the two of them both sitting up in bed. "See you later, then," she said before closing the door.

As she jogged down the stairs, grabbed her satchel and headed out the door, Starr wondered if this school year was going to be any different than last year.

Cole and Sasha Lester missing school activities.

Cole and Sasha Lester late to school activities.

Cole and Sasha Lester forgetting school activities.

Starr sighed as she smiled at Marcus and then climbed onto the backseat of the Bentley.

Her parents could really be a trip when they wanted to.

Starr kept eyeing her watch as she sat with her face in her hand as she doodled on her notebook and completely lost focus in her English class. It was hard to get lost in the pages of a book when she had her own minidrama unfolding before her. Her parents could be so embarrassing.

The parent-teacher conference wouldn't be big-time necessary if they had shown up for the school's open house this summer where parents were supposed to meet their children's teachers. That night a yacht party with Diddy had won out over open house at Pace.

Of course, they reasoned since she was a straight-A student that they were doing an oh-so-fabulous job. Not.

Starr sighed as she waited for Mr. Appleton to call her name and send her to the main office because her parents had arrived.

They better come through. They better.

"Starr, can I borrow a pencil, please?"

Rolling her eyes, Starr turned her head to look at KiKi Broner—daughter of a powerful software tycoon, whose breath smelled of onions and feet. "Listen, KiKi, tell your dad to buy you a Walgreens and then make sure you stock it with pencils and puh-lenty of gum," Starr finished snidely as she blocked her nostrils with her index finger.

KiKi looked offended as she threw up a hand in a retro diss and said, "Tell it to the hand." Starr just rolled her eyes again before she checked her watch and then shifted her eyes out the window.

Their appointment was for eleven o'clock and it was already past that.

Starr knew that the real reason she clowned on KiKi was her anger and hurt over her parent's no-show... again.

She was glad when the bell sounded and class was over. She hopped up from her chair, nearly knocking it backward as she rushed through the few students to step outside the door. She quickly reached for her BlackBerry and dialed her father's phone number.

Starr released an aggravated breath as she rolled her eyes. "Daddy, puh-leeze," she drawled. "Where are you?"

"About to go in the studio," he said simply.

"You forgot the meeting at the school!" she shrieked in pure frustration, drawing the curious stares of students lurking in the halls heading to their next period classes.

"Yeah, we forgot about that."

"Again," Starr stressed.

"I'm sorry, Starr, but we just found out Mary is on her way here. It couldn't be helped."

Starr sighed. "Where's Mama?"

"Right here. She's helping me produce this track and she might even sing on it."

And that made Starr freeze. What if she wants to strike up her singing career again? Her mother back in the studio? Between shopping and socializing, Sasha barely had enough time for Starr now. Back in the studio? Possible hit record? Touring?

She would NEVER see her mother.

"I just wish that you two would be just as interested in seeing *this* Starr as you are with hanging out with other stars. I need parents."

Starr flipped her phone closed.

Before she had time to drop it into her satchel it began to vibrate. "Let them get some of their own medicine," she thought, completely ignoring their calls.

twenty-one

Dionne
September 24 @ 11:50 a.m. | Mood: Determined

DIONNE was beyond grateful that her father did ante up the tuition but she was very aware that she wasn't helping his financial drama by always asking—and getting—expensive things. She figured that it was time for her to help out.

With one last pat to Linton's freshly braided hair, Dionne stood up from the steps and came around him to hold out one greasy hand for her pay. He slid the fifty-dollar bill to her without question and Dionne shoved it into the side pocket of her Gucci tote.

"Thanks, Dionne," Linton told her before he stood up and slid his red uniform blazer back on.

"No problem."

Dionne gathered her hair comb, brush and small jar

of hair grease into a plastic bag, tied it securely and then dropped it into her Gucci book satchel.

Between braiding hair in the hood and catching the few boys at school who didn't have fades, Dionne had already saved up five hundred dollars.

And she was quite proud of herself for not blowing it all on the cutest pair of Louboutins she saw at the mall yesterday.

Ding.

Dionne dug out her cell phone as she made her way across campus to the main building. Her stomach was straight growling and she only had ten minutes to scarf down lunch.

UR#1STARR: LOCATION???
DIVADIDI: ON MY WAY 2 CAF.
UR#1STARR: K.

Of course, Dionne had not clued the Pacesetters in on her side hustle. What would she say? *My big-time rapper daddy is going to go broke overspending so I'm helping out.* (HINT: She would never say that. *N-E-V-E-R!*)

Dionne was just glad she wore her oh-so-cute Louis Vuitton loafers with the cute little bows, dangling LV charm and cushioned insoles as she hurried up the steps of the main hall and down the long hallway to the rear of the building. She had no time to compare the comforts of the Pace Academy dining hall to Westside's prison-looking cafeteria as she zoomed over to the Little Italy pizza station and grabbed a veggie pan and bottle of fruit juice.

Starr frowned as she eyed her. "Really, Dionne, you are sweating like a pig. And why are your hands so shiny?" she asked as she tapped her pink glitter pen on the top of her netbook.

Dionne just shrugged as she rushed through her pizza. She barely had time to listen and for sure she had no time to talk. Over the rim of her clear plastic cup, Dionne paused at the sight of Marisol. Of course, she had seen her Latina best friend plenty all day, but Dionne still couldn't believe the…new Marisol.

No makeup on her already-pretty brown face.

No accessories to make her uniform stylish.

No ooh-aah curls in her hair, just a tight ponytail that looked completely product free.

Say what? Say who?

Not Marisol.

"Listen, ladies, I don't know what's going on with us, but we need to regroup," Starr told them as she leaned in. "Between this party and sniffing out the Diva of Dumb, I can't keep up with why you keep missing lunch, Dionne…and why you are in mourning or something, Marisol."

Dionne gave a quick glance at Marisol before she turned away.

The bell rang, signaling the end of the lunch period.

"Gotta run, girls. See you in art next period," Dionne told them before she grabbed her book satchel and hurried from the dining hall.

twenty-two

Starr
September 24 @ 4:20 p.m. | Mood: Like Kimora
(fabulous and in charge)

"**Thanks,** Marcus," Starr told her driver as he stood tall with the rear door of the Bentley open. She grabbed her things and stepped down onto the brick walkway leading to the side entrance of her twenty-thousand-square-foot house.

"Everything okay, Miss Starr?" he asked politely.

Starr nodded. "Yes, thank you," she lied without flinching. "See you in the a.m." *Like I'm going to unload my burden onto the shoulders of the help. Please.*

Starr noticed that both her father's newest Range Rover and her mother's customized pink Denali were not in their usual parking spots in the five-car garage. Just once it would be nice to come home and at least one of them was here, she thought, as she hurried inside the house.

Starr made her way straight to her bedroom suite. As soon as she crossed over the threshold she began to strip out of the uniform that she ab-so-lute-ly hated. She took a quick shower and wrapped a towel around her slender frame before heading to her walk-in closet. She grabbed both doorknobs and flung the doors open wide. The lights immediately came on.

Starr bit her bottom lip as she stood in the center of the room-size closet. She was in a problem-solving mood and she definitely wanted to channel the take-no-nonsense fabulousness of Kimora...but she didn't have time for her usual thirty-minute style session.

Being trapped in her dreary school uniform every day, Starr used any chance she could get to be fresh and fly. She had the kind of clothes most grown women would gnaw their foot off for. Might as well enjoy it.

With a sigh she snatched a navy linen Phillip Lim jumpsuit from one of the thousands of padded hangers. Since the front was a deep scoop neck, she grabbed a white ruffled camisole and a mix of pearls and long gold chains. Accessories were everything.

After moisturizing her entire body, spraying all her pulse points with Gucci Rush and removing the Gucci silk scarf she'd tied around her head during her shower, Starr dressed quickly. She was a woman on a mission.

PRIORITY LIST: 1) PARTY 2) FRIENDS 3) DIVA OF DUMB

Starr was the princess of lists. She sat down in her hot-pink leather chair. She opened her Mac, entered her password: DEATH2INTRUDERS.

Soon the rapid *CLICK-CLICK* of the keys echoed in her room as she updated TODAY'S TO-DO list:

HAVE NO CHOICE BUT TO DO LIST	JOB DONE	COMMENTS
★ Approve sketches of final decorations for party		Have 2 tell Daddy that the event stylist deserves a HUGE tip. LOVE, LOVE, LOVE it.
★ Double check thank you gifts arrived		The mini laptops are PER-FECTLY FABULOUS (just have to pre-load them w/ video of the party).
★ Check with Daddy for performers		So far seven acts confirmed. LUVS my Daddy. Ow!
★ Approve models for fashion show		No butt faces. Life is good. Lol.
★ Schedule fittings for models		Done and done.
★ Schedule dress rehearsal		Noon sharp @ venue.
★ Remind Daddy that camera crews are not a 24 hr thing		Waking up to a camera in your face while there is crust in your eye is just straight CRAZY. They will only tape the weekend's activities.

The Fierce and Fabulous Fashionista Fifteen party was definitely in cruise control at this point and Starr was big-time glad of that because she could not focus on anything else until the party was straight. With just a little over a week to go, Starr was ready to just chill and enjoy the weekend-long festivities—including a huge slumber/spa party in the pool house Friday night before the party and a brunch the Sunday after the party.

Starr crossed her arms over her chest as she leaned back in her chair. Next she was going to tackle Dionne and Marisol. Something was up with her gal pals.

Although Starr was not above holding on to a secret or two, she never thought they would keep secrets from her.

"I'll just kill two birds with one stone," she said aloud as she leaned forward to pick up her cordless.

She dialed Marisol's cell first.

"Hello."

Starr frowned at the sound of her voice. *What the…?*

"Starr?"

"Hold on. Let me get Dionne."

Starr dialed Dionne on three-way.

"Whaddup, Starr?"

Starr drummed her fingertips against the top of her desk. "Here's a better question: Whaddup with you two?"

The line remained quiet and Starr rolled her eyes, before she leaned forward to log on to Twitter. Starr's fingers flew across the keyboard as she sent a tweet/update to her 2,500 followers:

STARRLESTER: Getting annoyed w/ 2 best friends. Hate secrets. Uggh!

"Okay, Dionne, what's up with you missing lunch? You and Reggie finally making a connection?" Starr asked, as her eyes browsed the updates or "tweets" of the few people she followed on Twitter.

Dionne laughed. "Yeah, right."

Starr arched her perfectly groomed brow. "He's perfect for you."

"He's a'ight."

Starr frowned but she decided to stay on one road...for now. "So what's going on with you at lunch then?" she asked as she smiled at Diddy tweeting everyone to once again "LOCK IN."

"I've just been running late from my class. I guess I haven't recovered from lounging all summer because classes are getting to me now."

"Uhm, okay." The line went quiet.

"Marisol?" Starr prompted. "Why the fashion strike?"

Marisol sighed and Starr sat up a bit straighter, thinking she was about to get the real ish. "There's more important things in life than the who, what, when, where and why of clothes, Starr."

Starr's mouth fell open in shock.

"Sometimes I wish we were poor," Marisol added softly.

Starr nearly fainted and had to correct her slender frame from falling out of her chair.

"No you don't," Dionne threw in with attitude.

Marisol was as much a clothes fiend as she was. Something was up. *You don't go from oh-so-fab to downright drab...and like it???!!!* "Marisol, maybe you should lie down and go get a head massage because you're losing your mind," Starr snapped.

"No, I'm not," Marisol stressed. "Sometimes money is nothing but trouble."

"Puh-leeze," Dionne added.

Starr's brows almost furrowed into one line. "Oh, God, you're not going to stop wearing deodorant and grow dreadlocks, are you?"

Dionne laughed. "Starr, you stooopid."

Marisol sighed. "I gotta go. My mom needs me."

Seconds later the click let them know she had hung up.

"I gotta go, too, Starr. Call me when *106 & Park* comes on. My dad's gonna be on there."

Starr was too stunned over Marisol's abruptness to even speak.

Click.

Starr hung up the phone before her fingers flew across the keyboard. She hit Enter with a flourish.

STARRLESTER: Headed to the mall because I need some serious retail therapy. Gucci here I come. 4Real.

twenty-three

marisol never ever thought she would see the day that she hated her father's wealth and celebrity, but she was completely there now. In the days since the screening the atmosphere around their sprawling estate was awful.

Marisol's eyes were always looking up to God, praying that her family would make it through this.

Her mother's eyes were always red and puffy.

Her father's eyes were constantly looking anywhere but at his wife or his children.

Marisol hated it!

And she hated their money for drawing women to her father. She wanted so badly to pack up all her pretty designer things and give them away or throw them away.

"All of these women only want you for your name and

your money. You think if you had nothing all those women would throw themselves at you. You risk your family for that, Alex? I loved you when you had nothing."

And Marisol wished they had nothing because all the pretty things in the world meant nothing if her mother was hurting.

Marisol was rebelling against the fabulous life. She'd declared a moratorium on materialism. She just wasn't in the mood for it when it was the reason for her parents' drama.

Sighing, she left her bedroom suite and went to look for her mother. She found her on one of the balconies off the living room. Marisol forced herself to ignore the incredible view outside the French doors of their house.

Yasmine Rivera, glamorous in a DKNY burnt-orange cashmere sweaterdress and leather boots, looked over her shoulder and smiled softly at the sight of her daughter. Everything about her mom was perfect: the seemingly casual way she wore her hair, the makeup and the jewelry. It evoked an image of beauty and class.

"Come." Yasmine held her jeweled hand out while beckoning Marisol toward her with a nod.

Marisol came forward and slid her hand into her mother's as the quiet background of their beautifully landscaped estate surrounded them. Her mother slid her arms around her shoulders and hugged her close to her side. Marisol felt so many regrets. Mostly she wished that she had never eavesdropped on her parents' conversation. She got a glimpse into a part of their lives that she *never* wanted to see.

twenty-four

Dionne
September 25 @ 3:20 p.m. | Mood: Deceitful

Pace Academy definitely had a more laid-back atmosphere than any school she had ever attended before. It was so crazy to Dionne that the campus had fewer students than Westside but more land, more buildings, more everything. If she was honest with herself, it didn't seem fair at all.

Pulling her Louis V satchel higher up on her shoulder, Dionne shoved her hands into the hidden side pockets of her blazer as she made her way from the arts building to the main hall.

"Hey, Dionne, wait up."

She stopped and looked over her shoulder, her ponytail doing a semicircle around her head. She smiled at Reggie running to catch up with her. "What's up, Reggie?"

"You," he said as he came to a stop in front of her.

Dionne became a ball of nerves. She knew nothing at all about boys. Everything with Hassan just came naturally.

"I thought I could call you sometime," he said, not quite looking her in the eye as he shifted his hands from the straps of his book bag into the pocket of his gray pants.

Dionne pulled her side ponytail forward with her hand as she tilted her head to the side and smiled up at him. Reggie was her height with a dimpled grin and caramel skin with a light sprinkle of freckles across his nose. "Okay," was her simple reply before she turned and walked away.

"But what's your number?" he called after her.

Dionne turned again and walked backward. "That's for me to know and you to find out...if you want it bad enough."

He licked his lips and smiled as he shook his head just as Dionne turned and walked up the stone path leading to the main hall. As she made her way through the students at their lockers and on their way outside to their cars, Dionne remembered when things were simpler.

Hassan had walked up to her and flipped his phone open with his thumb poised and ready to get at the numbers. "What's your number?"

And she'd given up the digits just...like...that.

"Dionne, we're headed to Cooley's," Starr said, double-checking her appearance in the small mirror hanging from the door of her locker.

Dionne's eyes shifted to Marisol standing across the

hall at her own locker. "Mari, you going, too?" she asked, taking her Sidekick out to quickly text her mom.

DIVADIDI: MA, CAN I GO TO THE ICE CREAM SHOP W/ MARI AND STARR?

"I guess." Marisol just shrugged before she closed her locker and leaned against it.

Dionne watched several freshman boys walk by her and Marisol, turning to look over their shoulders at Mari. *They were probably wondering the same thing I am. Where is Marisol, the real Marisol? The flashy Marisol? The Marisol we're all used to.*

Ding.

DIDISMOM: CALLED THE DRIVER. BE HOME BY 6PM. SHARP DIONNE. LUV U.

Just as sure as Dionne knew her name she knew her mom was going to call her driver first. Dionne smiled. She was just glad her mama was in a good mood or whatever.

Starr eyed Dionne slipping her Sidekick inside her book satchel before she opened her locker. "Your mom said it was cool?" she asked.

Dionne shrugged, slightly embarrassed that she had to ask when Starr and Marisol did not.

Starr eyed Dionne as she touched up her lip gloss. "When are we going to meet your mom, Dionne?" she asked, pressing her lips together as she screwed the cap back on the tube of clear gloss with tiny gold flecks. *Glitzy indeed.*

Dionne felt like she just received a punch to the gut. "She's always so busy," she said, the excuse sounding lame even to her own ears.

Starr reached inside her locker for her new python-and-suede Gucci shoulder bag. "It's your turn to have a sleepover, you know…and not at your dad's all the time."

Dionne's stomach did somersaults after *that* one.

That old elementary school song came floating to her in a mocking childlike voice:

I was walking down the hall, when I felt something fall…diarrhea, diarrhea.

It fell down my leg like two scrambled eggs…diarrhea, diarrhea.

Dionne literally shook her head. "My dad's gonna buy us a bigger house—an even bigger house—and she's busy house-hunting right now," she lied. It was becoming easier and easier to lie with time and practice.

Marisol closed her locker, her book bag hanging from her shoulder. "Bigger house. Bigger troubles. Trust me."

Starr just sighed at Marisol's little bit of advice. "Really, Marisol, you are falling off."

Marisol looked at Starr. "So our friendship is based on what I wear?" she asked, snapping back.

Starr looked incredulous. "And that's new to you because…"

Uh-oh. Dionne stepped in between them. "Why are y'all trippin'?" she asked.

Marisol's full lips twitched. "I wouldn't want to embarrass you so I'll pass on the ice cream."

"Drama queen," Starr drawled before she slammed her locker.

"...*And* your stupid Fashionista Fool Fifteen party!" Marisol added over her shoulder before she walked down the hall and out the building like her pants were on fire.

"Marisol!" Dionne called after her, her voice echoing down the hallway.

"Jealousy doesn't look any better on you than the natural look," Starr flung back.

"Starr!" Dionne gasped, whirling to face her.

"What?" Starr asked innocently, looking completely unconcerned. She sucked her teeth and waved her hand dismissively. "Marisol will be fine. Like she's really gonna miss my party. Whateva. Let's go to Cooley's."

Dionne frowned. "Are you sure?"

Starr walked down the hall with her head held high like she was on a runway, leaving Dionne to follow.

Cooley's was *the* hangout spot for Pace Academy students. Besides great food—the *best* Reuben sandwiches—the atmosphere was made for teens, especially since the entire building was in the shape of a huge ice cream cone. The very sight of Cooley's made Dionne want to climb the cone and lick the swirl. The mood continued inside with its nearly all-white decor and music playing just loud enough to make it interesting.

Different cliques were gathered all over the restaurant, but everyone looked up and waved as Starr strolled inside. The girls slid into a cushy booth right by the door. "I wish Marisol was here," Dionne admitted as she scanned the menu.

"Well everyone else *is* here," Starr said, nudging the toe of her Gucci pumps against Dionne's red Vuitton loafer under the table as the front door opened. Jordan and the rest of his friends walked in.

Dionne watched Starr's eyes as they locked on Jordan and his crew as they all gathered at the tables in the center of the round-shaped restaurant.

Ding.

Dionne picked her Sidekick up from the white Formica table.

BIG REG: I wanted it and I got it.

Dionne looked up and found Reggie's eyes on her. He winked at her.

Starr grabbed the phone and read the text. "Do I smell *L-O-V-E* in the air?" she teased.

Dionne ignored her as she grabbed her phone back and worked her thumbs across the keyboard.

DIVADIDI: KEEP IT G-RATED PLZ. ☺

Their waitress came rolling over to them on her skates. Dionne ordered a Reuben with extra crispy fries. Starr ordered a banana split.

Jordan and Reggie arrived at their table before the food did.

"Hello, boys," Starr said, looking up at them with a big smile.

"Whassup?" Dionne added, feeling—like always—that she was in Starr's shadow.

The fellas eased down onto the booths.

Jordan slid next to Starr.

Reggie claimed the seat next to Dionne.

She fought the urge to move away from Reggie as his arm and thigh pressed against hers. And when he pressed a little closer she *didn't* fight the urge and scooted over to put precious inches in between them. *Good God!*

As everyone laughed and joked, Dionne fought hard to keep a smile on her face even as she thought, *I'd rather be with Hassan. 4Real.*

Ask and you shall receive.

Dionne grabbed her book bag and iPod from the rear seat of the car as her driver pulled to a stop in front of her apartment building. "Thanks," she said, her eyes locked on the sight of Hassan sitting on her front porch. "See you in the morning."

She walked up to him as the car pulled off, thinking he looked so cute in the colorful Coogi hoodie he wore with stiff jeans and black Uptowns. Her heart beat like crazy… just like always. "Hey, you," she greeted him with a smile.

Hassan turned and he smiled at her. It was a smile that expressed how happy he was to see her. "Only you could make that ugly uniform look fly," he told her with a laugh as he cupped his fist to his mouth.

Dionne playfully swatted his arm. "This is right off the Paris runways," she joked.

"Oh, okay. My bad. I respect your swagger, Ma."

Dionne sat down on the step next to him. It was so much easier to ignore Hassan by phone. In person she just loved being near him. She couldn't understand the who, what, when, where and why of it all. All she knew was what she felt—and being near Hassan made her feel good.

"There's a big welcome-back party at school," he said, turning his head to gaze at her. "I wanted you to go with me...if your mom will let you."

Yes! Her heart screamed.

No! Her mind battled.

"When is it?" she asked.

"Next Friday."

Starr's slumber party was the same night. Her face instantly filled with regret. "One of my friends from Pace is having a huge slumber party. Her dad's Cole Lester."

Hassan nodded as he shrugged his thin shoulders. "I guess you don't want to miss a party at Cole Lester's to go to a dumb party at Westside with me?"

His voice was an odd mix of sarcasm tinged with hope.

Dionne felt bad for letting him down, for ignoring his calls, for ignoring her heart. "Let's go to the movies," she suggested.

He smiled. "When, Saturday?"

"Well, her parents are throwing her a huge Fierce and Fabulous Fashionista Fifteen party," she told him, grabbing his wrist. "It's going to be just like all those parties on *My Super Sweet 16*. There'll be celebrities. A mad bunch of artists. Top-of-the-line everything."

She ran through all the details of Starr's party, including the invite party that was better than any party she'd ever been to. "I can't wait," she said excitedly.

Hassan's eyes got excited. "Wow, can I go?" he asked, only halfway sounding like he was joking.

Introduce Hassan to her fabulous life at Pace? No way. No how. He could blow everything...unless she admitted to him that she was faking like a Fouis Vuitton. And that was a big no.

"It's invite only. I'm sorry," she told him.

"That's cool." Hassan stood up and shoved his hands into the front pockets of his low-slung jeans.

Dionne looked up at him, wondering if he could see her heart pounding through her chest.

"Life is so different for you," he said, tilting his head to the side as he looked at her. "A lot of firsts that you'll never forget."

Dionne shrugged. "Yeah, I guess."

Hassan took his hands from his pockets and reached down to grab her hands to pull Dionne to her feet in front of him. "I know some of those preppy rich boys be hollerin' at you."

Dionne thought of Reggie.

Hassan lowered his head to Dionne. "You kissed any

of them yet?" he asked her softly, his words breezing across her lips.

Dionne shook her head as she looked up into Hassan's dark eyes just as the skies darkened with the approaching night.

Hassan pressed his soft lips to hers as his hands squeezed hers in the foot of space between them.

Her first kiss! Her first kiss!

Dionne completely forgot Reggie.

She let her eyes drift closed, counting the seconds so that she could put all the details in her journal.

When he stepped back from her, her eyes were still closed and her mouth was still puckered up like a fish.

Hassan laughed at her before he gave her hands one more squeeze. "A girl never forgets her first kiss," he said.

Dionne opened one eye just in time to see Hassan walking up the street and disappearing around a corner.

She released the breath she was holding as she touched her fingers to her tingling lips. She would never ever forget it.

twenty–five

Marisol
September 25 @ 8:13 p.m. | Mood: Hurt

MARISOL'S stomach growled as she pushed her history book away while sitting on her king-size bed. She fought the urge to ask one of the maids to bring her a snack and instead rolled over and flopped onto her back. She was contemplating whether to trudge all the way downstairs for a snack when her cell phone vibrated.

She picked it up from the two dozen silk pillows on her bed.

UR#1STARR: HAVE U PULLED THE STICK OUT UR BUTT YET?

Marisol rolled her eyes heavenward as she typed a response:

MARIMARI: HAVE U?
UR#1STARR: I FOUND UR STYLE. DO U WANT IT BACK?

MARIMARI: NO U USE IT. U NEED IT MORE.
UR#1STARR: ROTFL.

Marisol actually smiled. She and Starr had been friends since grade school. It was going to take more than one hallway squabble to wreck their friendship.

UR#1STARR: WHAT'S GOING ON WITH U? TELL ME. I'LL FIX IT.

Marisol didn't doubt that if Starr could fix it she would. But her parents' marriage was way out of Starr's reach.

MARIMARI: JUST SOME FAMILY DRAMA.
UR#1STARR: K. DON'T STRESS.
MARIMARI: THNX.

There was a knock at her door. "Marisol," her father called.

MARIMARI: GOTTA GO.
UR#1STARR: CALL ME LATER. GOT JUICE.
MARIMARI: ON WHO?
UR#1STARR: REGGIE ♥ DIONNE!!!
MARIMARI: O.M.G.

Marisol dropped her cell phone and climbed off her bed. She opened her door and leaned against it, blocking her dad from entering. She tried to look nonchalant, but she was mad at him.

"*Si, Papi?*"

He reached out to pull her ponytail. "Your mami mentioned you were in a little funk lately and I just wanted to come and make sure you're okay," he told her, in heavily accented Spanish.

How can you make sure I'm okay when you're the reason I'm not okay? "Just a lot of schoolwork," she lied. Schoolwork had never been a problem for Marisol. She'd been a straight-A student since grades really mattered.

Alex looked past his daughter to the open book on her bed. "Do you need a tutor?"

Marisol shook her head, just wanting him to leave before she started to cry like the time she completely missed going with her parents to France because she had a test. Then she remembered she wasn't supposed to care about stuff like that anymore.

Alex reached into the back pocket of his jeans and pulled out a gold money clip with his initials encrusted in diamonds. He peeled off several hundred-dollar bills from the wad of cash and handed them to her.

Marisol's immediate reaction was to take the money, but then she remembered her "death to materialism" pledge. She shook her head. "I don't need any more money," she told him, even as she thought of the shoes she could buy and bring home to introduce to her other shoes. Gucci python sandals meet Giuseppe studded thong sandal. Louboutin sequin heels meet Moschino velvet bootie. And so on. And so on.

Her father's expression was incredulous.

"I have a question maybe you can help me with," Marisol said suddenly, stepping back to allow him into her sanctuary.

Alex shoved the money back into his pocket as he walked in and sat down on one of the four vintage club chairs in the center of her room.

"I had really liked this boy—"

Alex jumped to his feet. "What boy?" he snapped, his eyes flashing against his light mocha complexion.

"Daddy, please," Marisol insisted as she sat down in the chair beside him, sliding her bare feet across the softness of the Oriental area rug.

"I found out that he had a girlfriend and he was lying to me," she finished, her eyes locked with his even though it was so hard not to look away.

Alex shifted uncomfortably in his chair.

"Why do boys lie and cheat?" she asked softly, wanting so badly to understand.

For a long time, Marisol and her father just looked at each other. She wondered if he could see her disappointment and hurt in her eyes. She knew she felt it every day in her heart.

"Those are things adults should deal with, Marisol. That's why I think you are too young, *mi hermosa,* to date." Alex walked to the door.

Marisol pulled her feet underneath her as she sat in the chair.

Her father paused in the open doorway, his head looking down at the floor. "Sometimes boys make mistakes, Marisol, mistakes that they regret."

With that he was gone. And Marisol felt relieved to be out of his presence. And that made her sad all over again, because before, she never thought anything could come between her and her father.

Marisol felt the tears well up in her eyes. She didn't stop them from falling as she jumped to her feet and dived into the center of her bed.

THE SECRET IS OUT!!
Posted in Good Gossip on September 26 @ 6:00 a.m. by thedivaofdish

I've never been very good at keeping secrets and seems like the new email addy I set up for hot tips is filled with other PA students who can't keep them as well.

There's some serious love in the air…just too bad a lot of it is on the low and based on some scandalous activity that would put their parents to shame. Seems like Heather and her "giving it up like coupons in a Sunday newspaper" crew have been B-U-S-Y.

Congrats to the lovebird. (Want photographic proof? Click on the link.)

Jordan and Heather
Ashton and Kimmie
Mark and Jess

On a side note: the usually ultra-fab Marisol Rivera has been on a bit of a strike lately. How long before Starrving for Attention boots her from their clique?

Only time will tell.
Smooches,
Pace Academy's Diva of Dish

155 comments

twenty-six

Starr
September 26 @ 7:45 a.m. | Mood: P-I-S-S-E-D!!

starr stared at the photo of Jordan and Heather hugged up—and definitely looking boo-ed up—until her eyes hurt. She tapped her thumb against the screen of her BlackBerry, wishing that it was really her fist punching Jordan and Heather's face, over and over and over again.

She forced herself to look out the window of the Bentley at the sprawling estates of Saddle River as she was whisked to school…just like any other morning.

But on any other morning her dream had not been shattered by the click of one stupid link, on one stupid blog, written by one stupid Diva of Dumb.

Starr fingered her diamond star-shaped pendant as disappointment flooded her in waves. Jordan—*her* Jordan—and Heather. The same Jordan who made her smile and laugh. The Jordan who gave her butterflies like crazy.

The Jordan who sang for her. The Jordan who she planned to ask to be her date for her party—and her very first kiss. The Jordan who she really thought liked her as much as she liked him.

Now that was all ruined because Jordan was a stupid, horny toad who couldn't turn down Heather, who was giving it away like free cheese.

Starr closed her eyes and made a fist as she forced herself to breathe deeply. "Boys are so stupid," she said in a low voice before tears welled up in her eyes.

She blinked them away as the Bentley pulled through the wrought-iron gates of Pace Academy. Starr slid on her Fendi square sunglasses, snuggled her black cashmere scarf around her neck, and smoothed her trembling hands over her short haircut and then down over her blazer-and-plaid-skirt uniform.

As soon as the Bentley pulled to a stop, Dionne and Marisol flew to the passenger door and flung it open before Marcus could even get out of the driver's seat.

"Ohmygod, ohmygod, ohmygod," Marisol kept repeating as she grabbed Starr's arm and nearly yanked her out of the car.

Starr wanted to slap her and almost did.

"Hush, Marisol. You sound like a parrot on crack," Dionne snapped, as she closed the door to the car.

Dionne had just saved Marisol's cheek—big-time.

Her friends got on either side of her and wrapped their arms around hers as they walked up the tree-lined stone path together.

"We've always heard rumors of Heather *doing the nasty*, but who knew it was true?" Dionne said, breaking their silence first. "And with Jordan."

Starr felt a deep pang of hurt. "Who knew his standards were so low," Starr drawled, glad that she sounded like this was just more of the Pacesetters' gossip and not such a devastating heartbreak for her.

"Heather probably pushed herself on him," Marisol added, before she uttered something under her breath in Spanish.

Starr arched a brow, but remained silent.

"Here comes Mr. Lover-Lover now," Dionne said.

The Pacesetters came to a stop. They all watched as nearly every student gathered on the massive front lawn eyed Jordan as he walked up to them. Time stood still for Pace Academy. Jordan was the center of attention.

"Starr, can I talk to you for a sec?" he asked, his eyes searching her as they were filled with... Regret? Shame? Guilt?

"I wouldn't want you to have to explain to your future baby mama why we're conversatin'...so I'll pass." Starr gave him a childish smirk before she continued walking, dragging Dionne and Marisol behind her.

Jordan reached out to grab her waist. "Starr, wait."

She pulled away from his hand, nearly smacking Dionne in the process. "Don't touch me. Don't you dare touch me, Jordan, with those hands that have been all up on *Hea-ther!*"

Jordan stepped back.

Dionne's eyes widened.

Marisol arched a slightly untrimmed brow.

Starr flushed with embarrassment before she composed herself, notched her head a bit higher and walked away.

"Thanks, Mimi," the three friends said as the uniform-clad maid handed each one a root beer float from the tray she carried.

The Pacesetters were lounging on the plush carpet of Starr's personal screening room as they went over every detail of Starr's upcoming birthday-weekend festivities. Starr was glad both her friends could stay over because thinking about Jordan and Heather was bumming her out big-time—not even the thought of the party was lifting her spirits.

"I hate that I have to leave so early in the morning but I am so excited to fly to Miami with my dad," Dionne said with the goofiest grin that made her face look like a huge toothy smile.

Marisol shook her head. "Tell your dad to beware of groupies, hoochies and goats," she said.

"Goats?" Dionne and Marisol exclaimed.

"Money is made of paper. Goats like paper. Beware of goats," she explained from behind her magazine.

Starr giggled because with Marisol's accent it sounded more like: Beeeware of goots.

"So…is anyone gonna talk about the elephant in the room?" Dionne said before taking a sip of her float.

Starr felt their eyes on her. "What?" she asked, trying to appear surprised.

"I've been holding on to this all day long," Dionne said, reaching up to twist her fine black hair into a loose topknot. "Why did you flip out like that on Jordan? Why was Jordan acting like he wanted to explain something to you? What is going on?"

Starr felt backed into a corner...but she wanted to talk about it. "I was going to ask Jordan to escort me to the party," she admitted, tucking the longest side of her hair behind her ear.

"You have a crush on Jordan?" Marisol gasped in surprise as she let her magazine drop to her lap.

Starr shrugged. "Doesn't really matter now, does it? Obviously what he's looking for I'm not giving up," she said.

Dionne and Marisol exchanged a look.

"So now the plan is to get an even bigger, even better escort," Starr told them, grabbing a pom-pom pen and her notepad. *To make Jordan sooooo mad.* "Suggestions, ladies?"

"Oooh. Souljah Boy," Dionne said right off the bat.

The girls paused, looked at each other with goofy smiles and then sang: "'*Hopped up out of the bed, turn my swag on...*'"

They burst into a fit of laughter, doubling over.

"Okay, ya'll, let's be serious about this."

"Okay, what about Bow-Wow?" Marisol said.

"Trey Songz."

"Cute but too old, Dionne," Starr responded as her pen flew across the paper.

"What about Yung Steff or Fabolous? You gotta have Fabolous for your Fab Fifteen!" said Marisol.

"Drake, please," Dionne said.

"Why not ask someone at the school?" Marisol offered.

"Or Quincy Brown?" Dionne said, falling back to fan herself with her hand.

The girls all took a moment to visualize the total cuteness that was Quincy—Diddy's stepson.

Starr scribbled *his* name twice and underlined it!

As the girls continued their playful banter, Starr's heart really wasn't in it. Truthfully, if the whole Heather thing had never gone down, Starr would've picked Jordan over *anyone* on the entire list in a heartbeat.

twenty-seven

Marisol
September 26 @ 6:45 p.m. | Mood: Spiteful

Marisol couldn't believe her mother had forced her to go shopping—and at the mall, no less. She loved Starr to death but she wasn't in the mood to buy her some fabulous birthday gift. She really wanted to give her something with more meaning to it than its hefty price tag. Maybe a gift certificate promising a lifetime of friendship?

The thought of Starr's reaction made Marisol smile. She bit her bottom lip and shook her tightly curled hair back from her face as she studied the jewelry display through the glass case at Bloomingdale's. She had browsed the entire store for every possible birthday gift she could think of for Starr and she just kept drawing a blank. Just as she had for the last few weeks, Marisol wondered what do you get for someone who has everything?

Yasmine walked up to stand next to her daughter. "Marisol, you go through this every year. Why do you drive yourself crazy over Starr's gift?"

Marisol shrugged. "I can never find the right thing," she admitted. "Will you help me?"

Yasmine hugged her daughter close to her side. "Wow, that's a first," she exclaimed.

"I'm going to check the shoe department and you look here," Marisol said, already walking across the store.

She really wanted to get away from the department store, having decided that whatever gift her mother selected would be the one Starr received in a pretty wrapped package. She loved her friend but she was big-time over the shopping.

Marisol used a band to pull her hair into a side ponytail as she walked out of Bloomie's and into the mall. Her heart slammed against her chest as she came to an immediate stop at the sight of Corey, her ex-crush, hugged up with some extra-tall and extra-thin blonde as they walked out of the movie theater. It had been a while since she had given him any thought, but seeing him with another girl just brought on all of her pent-up feelings and the hurt came crashing down.

In her eyes, he was a miniversion of her father—a cheat who didn't deserve to have a good time, a loser who needed to be put in his place.

Marisol arched her eyebrow as she watched them walking together and window-shopping. She stomped her flats against the tiled floor as she made her way over to them.

Corey looked like he unsuccessfully tried to swallow a tennis ball.

His boo (as in booboo the fool) eyed Marisol in a curious way. "Excuse us," she said sweetly, shifting to the left to try to move past Marisol politely.

Marisol stepped in front of Corey. "Is this the girlfriend you had when you were trying to get my number or is this another one?"

He glanced at the girl with him and then frowned. "Do I know you?" he asked, his eyes slightly mocking.

"So you're still trying to be a playa, huh?" she asked him as her stomach boiled with anger.

To her, Corey and her father were one and the same. She couldn't get all she had to say to her father off her chest, but she was going to unload on Corey the Cheat.

"Corey, who is she?" his girl asked.

Marisol shot her a brief look before shifting her eyes back to Corey, who was starting to look ill. "This has nothing to do with you…unless you don't care that your boyfriend is a lying, cheating, good-for-nothing whore who tried to holler at me while you two were together. Now if it doesn't bother you that your boo is a stupid cheater, that's your business. But trust and believe, he knows me and I sure know his loser behind. Isn't that right, Corey?"

"Come on, let's get out of here, Clarissa. This little girl is crazy," he said, hugging her closer as he attempted to move past Marisol as a crowd of onlookers began to stare.

Marisol blocked their path again, her eyes fiery as she went into full-throttle attitude mode: her Spanish accent became more pronounced, her finger wagging in his face with a little head rolling as well!

"You are an opportunist. You are a dog. You are stooooopid! You will grow up to be the worst kind of man, one who only cares about what he wants and doesn't give a scootie-boot-da-loop about who he hurts."

The onlookers began to applaud and Marisol looked around surprised by the number of people in the mall surrounding them. She hadn't even noticed them in her angry spiel.

She turned to a nervous-looking Clarissa. "Run while you can, Clarissa. Because whether you know it or not you have a dog on your tail."

With one last withering look at Corey that Starr would have rated an A+, Marisol hit Corey with her bag and then whirled around and pushed through the crowd.

Her heart was pounding in her chest.

Her face felt warm.

She felt more alive than she had in a long time.

She felt like throwing her fist up in the air like she was Rocky at the top of the steps in the movie.

She wished she could tell her father the exact same things.

She knew the pain she felt toward Corey could not compare with how her mother must feel, and Marisol wished she could make it all better for their family.

"Marisol, look what I found!" her mother exclaimed when she walked up to her still in the jewelry department.

Marisol barely took notice of the beautiful, chunky gold charm bracelet as she wrapped her arms around her mother's waist and hugged her tightly. "I love you very much, Mami," she whispered to her in Spanish as she inhaled deeply of her familiar perfume.

Yasmine returned the hug without question. "You really like the charm bracelet that much?" she asked.

Marisol couldn't have cared less about the charm bracelet. In that moment she just wanted her mother to know that she was loved. Big-time.

twenty-eight

Dionne
September 27 @ 10:45 a.m. | Mood: Excited

DIONNE had been glad to climb out of the SUV and into the chartered private jet at six in the morning. After a late night with her girls, the early morning start was testing her stamina. All she wanted to do was cuddle in one of the plush leather seats and sleep—just like her Pops and the entire eight-man crew.

She'd been just as happy for the jet to land in Miami. She was ready to experience the party city to the fullest. Well, as much as she could at fifteen.

Dionne paused at the top of the steps as she slid on her aviator sunglasses and let the Miami wind blow her jet-black hair.

"Come on, baby girl," her dad said at the foot of the steps of the plane.

Dionne threw him her best daddy's-girl smile as she

jogged down the steps to the tarmac and climbed into the Cadillac Escalade ahead of him. Dionne knew she was smiling like a fool and she didn't care one bit. Spending the entire weekend with her dad *and* being on a private jet *and* getting to see a real video shot was fabulous. Life was *so* good right now.

"Dionne, call your mama and let her know we landed safe," Lahron told her as Mindy, his personal assistant, handed him yet another BlackBerry for yet another business call.

Dionne dug into her red patent leather embossed Louis V tote for her cell phone and dialed away since she knew her mother was worrying. She had her proof when the phone barely rang. "Ma?"

"Hey, baby girl."

Dionne smiled. "We're in Miami. We just landed."

"Good."

Dionne looked out the window at the stretch of palm trees. "Don't worry. 'Kay?"

"Okay. Just have fun. Be safe. And don't wander off alone, Dionne."

"I love you, Ma."

"Love you, too."

While her father took phone calls left and right, Dionne just sat on the edge of her seat and enjoyed the beautiful view of Miami. She couldn't lie. She was having a ball being spoiled. Living with one foot in the fabulous world really got to her at times. She loved her mom and she knew her mom loved her. But the difference in her life Monday through Thursday with her mom, and Friday through Sunday with her dad was obvious.

As they walked into their penthouse suite at The Palms, Dionne felt like she was the lead in some swaggerific video as she looked past the plush furnishings to the private terrace overlooking the ocean.

"Mindy, show my daughter her room and let her order whatever she wants to eat," Lahron instructed his assistant before using the remote to turn the surround system on. Soon the sounds of his newest single filled the air.

"You hungry?" Mindy asked, looking more and more out of place in her father's hip-hop world.

"Starving," Dionne admitted as she followed Mindy into her bedroom. "Just a salad and cheeseburger would be good."

"Coming right up."

Dionne was happy when Mindy left her alone. She quickly unpacked her clothes and took a quick shower before she changed into a striped bikini with a bandeau top and low-slung bottoms that tied at the sides. Her mama would have made her wear a cover-up. "Mama ain't here," she sang, checking her appearance in the mirror as she put on large gold hoop earrings and twisted her hair up into a messy topknot.

She opened the door and paused at all the activity in the suite. She had barely made it into the hall when her father came walking toward her. "Let me holler at you, Dionne," he said, breezing past her to walk into her bedroom.

"Yes, Daddy," she said, closing the door behind them.

"Where's the rest of your bathing suit?" he asked, removing his shades to look at her.

Say what? Say who?

Dionne looked down at herself. "There isn't any more," she explained.

Daddy never flexes.

"Did my mama call you?"

Lahron the Don in all his blinged-out gloriousness reached in the front pocket of his loose-fitting seersucker shorts for a wad of money. "First put on some clothes. Then burn that bathing suit. Then go shopping to buy you another one. A one-piece."

Dionne's eyes widened. "But Daddy—"

"But Daddy hell," he said in a stern voice as he gave her the once-over. "In life, men judge you by appearances. It ain't right, but it is what it is. The most important thing a woman has is her reputation. Don't be in a rush to grow up, Dionne. You hear me?"

She nodded as he hugged her close to his side and pressed money into one of her hands. "Let Mindy take you shopping," he told her.

Dionne shook her head. "I have other bathing suits, Daddy. I'll just wear one of those," she told him, pushing the money back into his hand. Thoughts of him blowing all his money still plagued her.

Lahron tilted his head back to laugh, exposing his diamond grills. "Since when do you say no to shopping?" he joked.

Dionne just smiled and hugged him close. "You don't

have to buy me all that expensive stuff all the time, Daddy. I'm just happy to hang out with you."

Lahron leaned back to look down at her. "You mean that, don't you?" he asked, sounding surprised.

Dionne nodded.

"I just want to give you everything I couldn't have," he said.

"Don't get me wrong, I like those nice things, but I don't need them to spend time with you," she said honestly.

"In this business it seem like everybody want something from you, baby girl. You just don't know," he said, sounding sad.

Her heart tugged for him. She really had no idea how it felt to be him—to go from struggling and hustling to making a lot of money. She didn't know everything her daddy had to put up with. She watched enough TV and read enough gossip blogs to know that the music industry and those in it could be crazy.

"You always got me, Daddy," she promised him. "No matter what, you got me and I got you."

twenty—nine

Marisol
September 29 @ 7:45 a.m. | Mood: Bored

Marisol took the iced mocha coffee topped with whipped cream that Dionne handed to her. Because it was from McDonald's and not Starbucks, Marisol didn't feel so bad about the indulgence.

"I have the Diva of Dumb narrowed down to three people," Starr said, pacing the length of the bathroom as she, too, took a deep sip of her frothy drink.

"You really are on a mission," Dionne drawled, as she flipped her newly relaxed hair over her shoulder.

If looks could kill, Marisol was sure Starr would've dropped Dionne where she sat.

"Not a mission, Dionne. This is war. She, he or he-she started it, and we're going to finish it."

Dionne nodded.

The outside door to the bathroom opened and the

three girls whipped their heads around to see who would dare enter.

Peyton Parker strolled in with all her bleached-blond glory. The junior's father was a hedge-fund manager who was rumored to be swindling millions from his clients. Yet, Parker walked around like she didn't have a care in the world.

Starr stepped forward as she eyed Peyton. "Excuse me, but the sign on the door is not a mistake," she snapped.

Peyton frowned. "Look, I have to pee. I don't care about your stupid little Pacesetter meeting, Starr," she said, sounding bored as she tried to move forward.

Starr stepped in her path.

Marisol and Dionne stepped on either side of her.

"Are you three serious?" she said, stepping back.

The Pacesetters stepped forward and crossed their arms over their small chests.

"You don't own Pace Academy, Starr."

The girls said nothing and moments later a pitiful-looking Peyton turned and left.

"So, any-way," Starr said as they all resumed their positions pre-intrusion. "There's Monica Julius, Jennifer Hartan and Franklin Franklin—side note, his parents are dead wrong."

Marisol frowned. "Who are they?"

"Exactly," Starr stressed.

"Huh?" Dionne and Marisol said in unison.

"None of them were invited to my party. They are all

computer geeks who already have blogs, and word is they resent—and I quote—'the ostentatious display of wealth here at Pace Academy.'"

Dionne licked the extra whip cream from her mouth. "Then why go here? Everyone knows Pace is what it is and there are plenty of people who would love to get in."

"You have to admit that everything at Pace is over the top. It can be hard to swallow," Marisol told them. "Money *isn't* everything."

Starr rolled her eyes. "I don't like labels—"

Unless they're designer, Marisol thought as she stirred her drink with her straw.

"But these three are complete losers who would want to take me down," Starr finished, ignoring Marisol.

The first bell rang.

The girls gathered up their book bags and tossed the rest of their beverages into the trash bin before walking out of the restroom. Marisol grabbed their sign and handed it to Starr to slide in her satchel.

Beeeep.

"Attention all faculty and students. Please report to the auditorium for a first-period assembly."

Marisol felt relieved. "Thank God. I was not in the mood for my algebra class anyway."

The girls made their way down the hall to the auditorium.

"Wonder what this is all about?" Starr asked as they claimed seats at the rear of the auditorium.

"Hi, girls."

All three looked up to find Heather waving at them from a few rows in front of them. They ignored her.

Heather's face looked sad before she turned around.

Marisol actually felt sorry for her. Heather had officially been labeled and no matter what she did, many students at Pace would never let her forget it.

Jordan and his friends came in and Marisol's eyes shifted to Starr. She didn't miss the hurt she saw in her friend's eyes. The same hurt she felt about Corey. Boys *S-U-C-K* big-time.

Marisol reached past Dionne to squeeze Starr's hand and offer her a smile.

"Quiet down, students. Quiet down!"

Marisol crossed her legs, pulling her plaid skirt down over her knees, as she locked her eyes on Headmaster Payne standing onstage.

"Good morning, students," he said into the microphone, as he wiped his bald head with his hand.

"Good morning, Headmaster Payne," the entire assembly greeted him in return.

He cleared his throat. "Based on the survey conducted by students and parents at the end of the last school term, the board of trustees has decided—"

"Why does he always look like he just ran a marathon in his suits?" Starr whispered.

"—to revise the policy on uniforms by making them optional effective immediately," said Headmaster Payne, finishing up his announcement as he pulled a handkerchief from his pocket to wipe his upper lip.

The entire auditorium erupted in thunderous applause and many students jumped to their feet.

Starr and Dionne punched their fists in the air. "Oh, it's on now!" Starr assured them. "Watch your girl's shoe game now. Just watch it."

"Quiet down, students. Quiet down."

Everyone settled into their seats but there was still an air of excitement.

"In homeroom you will receive the revised student handbooks with the new dress code for Pace Academy and I strongly advise you to avoid any infractions," the headmaster continued. "Ladies and gentlemen, remember that first impressions are important. Be mindful of the image you present."

Over the rim of his glasses, Headmaster Payne's eyes swept from the left to the right of the auditorium as if giving each and every student a stern look. "Assembly is dismissed."

Marisol grabbed her Coach wristlet—a small luxury she allowed herself over the huge designer totes she used to love—and followed an excited Dionne and Starr out of the auditorium. *Just my luck,* she thought. *They finally get rid of uniforms while I'm on a fabulous strike!*

Marisol rolled onto her side as she lay in bed. She looked up at the full moon through the windows, wishing she could sleep...but it was hard when her parents were arguing.

"Leave, Alex! Just go."

Marisol closed her eyes and curled into the fetal position in the middle of her bed.

Things between her parents were getting worse. She wanted to be home with her family, but at the same time she wanted to be free of the tension she felt there.

Tears welled up in her eyes again as she thought of the constant bickering and the growing distance between her parents. The way they passed each other in the hall, making sure neither touched the other. She'd even caught her father sneaking into the house in the middle of the night to sleep in one of the guest bedrooms.

Marisol buried her face into the down pillows as she tried to soothe away her own tears.

"I am so sick of your lies, Alex."

"Lower your voice, Yasmine. You'll wake the children."

Marisol reached out and grabbed her cell phone from the glass-topped nightstand. The phone illuminated as she flipped it open. She quickly dialed.

"Marisol? Marisol?" Starr said, sleep heavy in her voice. "What's wrong?"

"I think my parents are getting a divorce," she admitted in a whisper. *There. I said it.*

"Oh, Mari," Starr sighed pitifully.

It only made Marisol cry harder.

"Is that why you been looking and acting depressed lately?" Starr asked.

Marisol reached under the silk Gucci scarf tied around her head to scratch her scalp. She flopped over onto her back and wiped the tears from her eyes with the back of her hands as she looked at the huge crystal chandelier hanging from the ceiling.

"Why didn't you tell us, Mari?" Starr asked.

"I didn't want to talk about it," she admitted, thankful that her parents' argument had ended or at least quieted down enough to not escape the walls of their suite.

"Then we won't talk about it," Starr assured her. "Hold on. I'm calling Dionne."

Click.

"Whassup?"

"What are you wearing to school tomorrow?" Starr asked, sounding more like a perky cheerleader than a laid-back style diva.

"Are you two *that* excited about no uniforms tomorrow?" Dionne joked. "It's after midnight."

"I'm sending you two a picture of my outfit all laid out." Starr told them. "Oh, your girl will be best dressed."

"Oh…okay. Let me go back in my closet."

"Both of you just be glad I'm on strike," Marisol tossed in.

The girls continued their playful banter and Marisol was grateful for the obvious diversion. What would she do without her friends?

thirty

Dionne
October 2 @ 7:30 p.m. | Mood: Happy

DIONNE loved hanging out with her great-grandmother on her mother's side. Mama Belle was funny but would get serious in a heartbeat. She loved the Lord and going to church but she could flip and curse a fool out without batting an eye. She was loving and affectionate, but she would whip some behind if one of her grandkids went to the wrong side of crazy.

"There go my Didi just as cute as me," Mama Belle said as soon as they walked through the front door of her small three-bedroom house in Irvington.

Didi went right to Mama Belle and hugged her close as she sat in her beloved recliner that she kept stationed by one of the living-room windows. "Hey, Mama Belle."

"Mama Belle, you need to turn down your heat,"

Risha complained as she peeled off the short jacket she wore with jeans.

"Well, you can slip that lil' jacket right back on because we headed to Route 22," Mama Belle said, rising to her full almost six-foot height.

Dionne froze. She loved her Mama Belle, maybe even more than her grandmother who lived in North Carolina. But she knew a shopping adventure with Mama Belle meant some clothes for her.

The thing was, Mama Belle swore by three stores when it came to shopping: Walmart, Kmart and Target. That was it.

Uh-oh. Dionne cut her eyes over at her mama, who was smiling like, "Yup, let's go."

As they filed back out into the fall air, Dionne said a silent prayer that Mama Belle stuck to the housewares section of the store and left the juniors department alone.

"Didi, your mama tells me you don't have to wear uniforms to that fancy school your daddy sends you to—"

Didi's stomach bubbled.

"So Mama Belle gon' buy her baby some clothes."

Didi felt like she could flatline right there. Boom. Hit the floor. No coming back.

"That's okay—"

Dionne pressed her lips all the way together when Mama gave her "the look" as they climbed into the car. The last time she tried to turn down Mama Belle's Kmart offerings her mama had forced her to wear them and confiscated all the clothes her father had bought.

"Thanks, Mama Belle," Didi said, definitely not wanting a repeat of that incident.

Dionne's bedroom door opened and she looked up from her spot on the floor to see her mother standing in the doorway. "You know you're going to wear those clothes, right?"

"I know."

Risha walked into the room and sat down on the bed, watching Dionne as she pulled the clothes from the plastic bag and put them on hangers. "There was a time when all you wore was Walmart and Old Navy or GAP clearance. I talk to you all the time about not letting your daddy's money go to your head, Dionne. You were perfectly fine before Pace Academy. You don't have to pretend to be someone else."

"I know," Dionne said again.

Risha reached down and picked up a khaki camp shirt. "This is cute and I bet if I sew a designer label in it you and your little crew at Pace would snatch it up and pay ten times what your Mama Belle paid."

Dionne smiled up at her mom as she peeled the black paint from her index finger. "That's true."

Risha got down on the floor next to her daughter. "Now if you take this shirt and white tank with those two-hundred-dollar jeans your daddy buys, with your shoes and your designer bags, no one would ever know this is a seven-dollar shirt."

Dionne visualized the outfit. "So just mix it up, huh?"

Risha leaned over to bump her shoulder against her daughter's. "Girl, I thought all those fashion magazines y'all read woulda taught you how to do that."

Dionne laughed.

"You better now? No more moping in your room?" Risha asked, rising to her feet as her earrings went *clang-clang.*

Dionne realized she was acting like a brat. She was gone a lot of weekends and she usually spent time hanging out with her mother during the week. Tonight she went straight to her room as soon as they got home.

"I'm good," Dionne said, looking up at her with a genuine smile.

Risha reached out with her fist. "Love you," she said.

Didi made a fist and lightly touched it to her mom's. "Love you more."

thirty-one

Starr
October 2 @ 7:30 a.m. | Mood: FABULOUS!

Starr loved, loved, loved that Pace Academy was a complete and total fashion battleground. And she was making it her business to be the biz-ness every single day.

As her chauffeured Bentley pulled up to their usual meeting spot, Starr checked Marisol and Dionne out through the tinted glass. She shook her head upon seeing Marisol still wearing the old Pace uniform—she gave her friend a bye since she was in the throes of family drama. Shifting her eyes to Dionne, Starr nodded in approval at the casual yet chic look she sported. Dark denim jacket. Stark white fitted tee. Linen maxi-skirt. She accessorized with a mix of a half-dozen gold, turquoise and jade long chains in varying lengths. The Michael Kors platform gladiator sandals and a huge orange patent leather Valentino bag—the bright colors worked well with her mocha complexion.

Although there was a nip in the air and the sun wasn't one hundred percent, Star slid on her shades and climbed from the Bentley as Marcus held her door. Starr flipped her long bangs from her face as she slid her tote onto her arm. "Thank you, Marcus," she told him before strutting over to her waiting friends.

"Have a good birthday, Miss Starr."

"I will," she told him with a huge grin.

Moments later the vehicle pulled away.

"Happy birthday, Starr!" Dionne and Marisol screamed before they both hugged her close.

"Thank you. Thank you." Starr did a little curtsey once her friends released her.

"Starr, your outfit looks even better in person than it did on iChat," Dionne told her.

Starr couldn't agree more.

The charcoal wool skinny pants, leather-heeled booties and a light gray silk shirt were set off by a lightweight, charcoal wool oversize sweater that flared just a bit around her knees with the collar flipped up. Onyx chains and oversize rings accessorized the outfit.

She knew the look was a bit much for school, but Starr loved being a bit much—especially on *her* day. Loved it!

Ding.

Starr reached in her crocodile Prada bowler bag for her cell. She rolled her eyes at yet another person texting her for tickets to the party. "I have to change my number…again," Starr told them as they walked up the stone path to the main hall.

"Starr, you have to understand that *no one* wants to miss your party this weekend," Dionne told her before sliding her aviators up on her forehead, pushing back her Pocahontas-styled hair.

"I know," Starr said with a huge grin. "Heck, I don't want to miss it myself."

They laughed as they made their way inside the main hall to their lockers. Starr paused at the sight of a huge crystal vase of pink roses sitting in front of her locker.

"Ohmygod, they're be-oooooo-tee-ful," Marisol sighed as she bent down to pick them up and then shoved them into Starr's hands—which wasn't easy since the arrangement was tall enough to sit in the foyer of a mansion.

Several students gathered around them.

"Thank God there're no thorns," Starr drawled jokingly as she reached in with black painted nails for the card.

"Who's it from, Starr?" Dionne asked excitedly.

Jordan, Starr thought, as she removed her shades. *They have to be from Jordan.*

She opened the black envelope and her smile faded just a little bit. She cleared her throat:

To our Baby Girl, we hope you have a birthday
that is as beautiful and fabulous as you are.
—Love Always, Mommy & Daddy

As the girls in the hall of Pace Academy all oohed and aahed over the flowers, Starr let the disappointment of them not being from Jordan settle around her shoulders.

Ever since that day she screamed on him, Jordan had left her alone. No e-mails. No texts. No funny jokes. No more dropping by her house to chill. No stopping by to speak when he had to go to the studio with her dad. Barely a smile in the hall when they passed.

They never made it to girlfriend-boyfriend and now even their friendship was big-time over…and she missed him.

Starr was completely exhausted by the end of the school day. So many people had given her cards and gifts for her birthday that she felt bad about not inviting them—and so the count for the party swelled by another twenty-five.

Marcus's arms were loaded as he carried the brightly wrapped gifts into the foyer for her. "Had a good day, huh?" he joked.

"Call me Tony the Tiger, 'cause I had a *grrrreat* day."

Starr made her way over to the intercom system. "Mimi, there're some presents on the foyer table, could you put them with the rest of the gifts?" she asked politely, before heading across the sunken two-thousand-square-foot living room and up the marble stairs to her suite.

The scent of her room was a mixture of Gucci perfume and the strawberry essence of her huge scented candles. She kicked off her heels, dropped her purse by the door, and plopped down in her hot-pink-and-white paisley chaise longue by the French doors.

Tonight her father was taking the entire family to one

of her favorite New York restaurants, Bungalow 8, for dinner and Starr had just a few hours to put together an outfit.

Starr walked over to her desk and pushed the intercom button. "Mimi, are my parents home yet?" she asked, dropping down into her chair.

"Not yet."

Starr picked up her cordless and called her father's private cell phone.

"Whaddup, birthday girl?"

Starr smiled. "Nothing much, Daddy. Mama and the twins with you?" she asked as she propped the phone between her ear and shoulder as she logged on to her computer.

"Yes, we're on the way home now."

Starr closed her eyes as relief flooded her. She half expected them to say they were off to some party or some meeting or some red-carpet walk-through and would miss spending her birthday with her. It's not like she had never been disappointed before.

"Are we still going to Bungalow 8?" she asked, tensing again.

"Yes."

"Okay. Good."

As soon as Starr placed the cordless back in its charger there was a knock at her door. "Come in," she called out, as she logged in to her MySpace, Facebook, Twitter, Ning, AIM and e-mail accounts.

Mimi walked in holding a huge white box with a hot-pink bow.

"Another gift? It can go with the rest of them in the media room, Mimi," Starr told her over her shoulder.

"It's from Jordan," Mimi said, sitting it on the end of Starr's bed.

Starr's heart stopped and then went back to beating full force. She shrugged. "I'll open it later," she said, pretending to focus on the computer screen.

As soon as Mimi left the room, closing the door behind her, Starr whirled in her chair to eye the box. For the longest time she stared at it sitting there, forcing herself to go about the rest of her routine. She answered e-mails. Tweeted. Showered. Moisturized. Did her makeup. Dressed.

And as she stood in the doorway of her room, with her finger poised at the light switch, she eyed it once more before turning off the light, bathing the room and the gift in darkness.

thirty-two

Dionne
October 3 @ 7:45 p.m. | Mood: Excited

DING.

Dionne snatched her cell phone up from the counter-top where she was sitting with Marisol along with the twenty other giggling, terry-cloth-robe-wearing girls scattered around the pool house.

BIG REG: SEND PICS OF THE SLUMBER PARTY.
DIVADIDI: STOP BEING A PERV.
BIG REG: IM UR PERV.
DIVADIDI: FAIL.

Dionne frowned and tossed her cell phone back onto her tote bag. Reggie was beginning to work her nerves with his corny double-talk. After a week of talking to him on the phone, most of his conversations revolved around body parts. And now he wanted her to send him photos of girls—probably hoping they were in their nightgowns. Uggh!

"Okay, ladies, focus."

All eyes turned to Starr as she stood up at the front of the living room of the guesthouse wearing the only hot-pink terry-cloth robe in the house. "Thank you all for coming to my pre-Fierce and Fabulous Fashionista Fifteen birthday slumber/spa party!"

All the girls clapped; most were glad to just be a part of Starr's fabulous inner circle.

Dionne smiled and shook her head at the way Starr was so obviously aware of the two cameramen in the room as they caught every moment of the weekend-long festivities.

"You having fun, girls?" Starr's mom, Sasha, asked as she walked into the guesthouse through the rear patio doors looking laid-back and casually fabulous in a white flowing sundress that showed off the tattoo on her shoulder. Her hair was pulled back in a sleek ponytail, with shades and trendy jewelry.

"Yes, Mrs. Lester," Dionne told her after accepting a quick hug. Honestly, Dionne was still completely star-struck by Sasha Lester. She used to sing into a hairbrush to the songs she made famous.

Marisol accepted a brief hug, as well. "Even though I am trying to shed the trappings of wealth, I am having fun," she admitted with a dimpled grin.

Sasha Lester removed her shades as she looked down

at Marisol. "Say what? Say who?" she asked, with a funny expression.

Dionne covered her laugh with her hand. "It's a long story, Mrs. Lester," she told her. "But Marisol is on a strike against fabulous. Go figure."

Sasha eyed Marisol again before she patted her cheek and moved past her to reach Starr. A lot of the girls whispered excitedly at the sight of Sasha Lester.

"Hello, ladies. Welcome. Welcome. Our home is your home. I just wanted to welcome you and tell you all to have a good time. If there is anything you need just let me or one of the staff know, okay?"

Sasha gave Starr a kiss on the forehead, whispered something in her ear and then waved at the girls once more before she left through the front door of the guesthouse.

Ten uniformed attendants filed into the guesthouse.

"Okay, ladies, spa stations have been set up in the rooms for you to enjoy," Starr announced, completely secure in her element and the center of attention. "Several types of mani-pedis are available in room one, deep stone massages in room two, and eyebrow waxing and threading in room three and the Jacuzzi is just outside the back door. There are several staffers floating around to take your drink and food orders. Enjoy!"

Dionne smiled contentedly at the fun her friends were having. Starr made her way over to them, stopping to chitchat with everyone like a teen socialite. "Did you open Jordan's gift yet?" she whispered to Starr, letting curiosity get the better of her.

Starr shook her. "The only thing on my mind is a chocolate mani-pedi for me and an eyebrow wax for Marisol."

Marisol gasped as if she was offended.

"I mean really, Mari, if you don't do something you're gonna be able to play Ugly Betty with that freaking caterpillar unibrow," Starr snapped.

Marisol turned to Dionne for support.

Dionne could only nod her head in agreement before she took her index finger and laid it across her own brows to connect them. Marisol swatted her arm.

"Ow!" Dionne rubbed the spot that still stung.

Marisol stopped a server carrying a tray and grabbed a flute of something frozen and fruity.

"Come on, Marisol, you really are a bigger diva than Starr," Dionne told her.

"Hey." It was Starr's turn to sound offended.

"Tell me you don't miss all your pretty clothes and shoes and makeup and jewelry and spa treatments."

Marisol shook her head. "I don't miss it. Life is so much simpler. Be-leeve me. But for you, Starr, I will be a good guest and enjoy these material things."

Marisol walked away with her head held high.

Starr and Dionne were thankful she carried herself into the room to get her eyebrows cleaned up.

"Who does she think she's fooling? She knows she misses being pampered," Starr smirked before walking off.

Dionne glanced down at her phone on top of her tote. Tonight was the night of the party Hassan asked her to attend. Biting her bottom lip, she grabbed her phone and walked out the rear doors of the guesthouse. She quickly dialed his cell phone number.

It seemed to ring endlessly.

"I'm not callin' you no more, Dionne, and if you take too long to call me I'm not gonna answer."

She touched her lips, remembering the sweet feel of Hassan's lips on hers. She hadn't heard from him since.

A kiss goodbye?

Taking full advantage of her Pacesetter status—something she normally didn't do—Dionne jumped the line for the deep stone massages. She suddenly needed one really, really badly.

thirty-three

Marisol
October 3 @ 10:45 p.m. | Mood: Bummed

Marisol eased out of her theater seat.

"Marisol, where are you going?" Starr whispered to her in the darkness as she lightly grabbed her hand.

"I'll be right back," she whispered, bending down some so that she didn't block the movie screen as she hightailed it out of there.

Marisol tripped.

"Ow!" someone hollered out.

"Sorry," Marisol said over her shoulder before she finally stepped out into the hall.

She felt like a bird freed from its cage.

In truth the media room reminded her too much of the night her view of her parents' relationship changed forever—and that was something she wanted to forget.

She didn't even watch the broadcast of the documentary when it aired on ESPN.

Flipping her phone open, Marisol dialed her mom.

"*Hola,* Marisol," her mother answered speaking in Spanish.

She smiled at the happiness she heard in her mother's voice. Too bad it was as fake as fifty-dollar Gucci bags (like, who really believed *those* were real?). "I was just checking up on you."

"Marisol, I am the mother. I do the worrying, not you."

Marisol walked outside the Lesters' mini-movie theater that included a well-lit marquee, a robotic ticket taker and a concession stand. "Where's Papi?" she asked.

"In his office."

Marisol crossed her arms over her chest as she hopped on the elevator and rode it up to the first floor.

"Something wrong, Marisol?" Yasmine asked in fluent and rapid Spanish. "Why aren't you enjoying Starr's party?"

"I just missed you, that's all," Marisol said, stepping off the elevator into a small hallway off the recreation room.

Yasmine laughed.

It sounded pleasant and that made Marisol feel better.

"I've noticed that you've been a little down lately, Marisol. And I just want you to be a teenager and enjoy yourself. Please."

Marisol nodded even though her mother couldn't see her. "*Sí, Mami.*"

"Now, tell Starr and Dionne I said hello and have fun, little girl."

Marisol said goodbye and flipped her phone closed. She walked across the rec room and out onto the lighted stone patio. The October air was chilly at night and Marisol was grateful for her oversize flannel pajamas and cow-shaped slippers—both of which Starr promised to burn the first chance she got. She inhaled a deep breath of the night air and immediately felt refreshed.

She paused in the doorway and looked up at the sight of the moon in the sky. It was beautiful and serene.

Marisol walked out onto the patio. Bright colors flashed in her corner vision. She was surprised to see Mrs. Lester stretched out on a lounge chair with a fur blanket across her legs and a fuzzy neon-green sweater on. Her eyes were closed.

Marisol turned to go back through the door.

"Just the little girl I wanted to see," Sasha said.

Marisol froze before she turned to face her.

Sasha sat up and patted the empty lounge chair next to her. "Come on and tell me 'bout this strike you're on," she prompted.

Marisol shrugged as she dropped down onto the chair. "I just think there are more important things—like family and loyalty and trust and friendship—that's more important than what designer I'm wearing or if I got a spa treatment this week."

"You know I've known you a long time, Marisol. You and my baby have been friends since first grade at Pace

Academy." Sasha smiled. "And I can't ever remember you not just *being* fabulous and feisty and all of that, but also not *enjoying* it. It's a part of what makes you who you are. I think you've been wearing lip gloss since you were in third grade."

Marisol laughed at the memory. "My mami was so mad at me when I came home with those red lips."

"Humph. I don't blame her."

They fell silent.

"Don't be mad but Starr told me a little bit about your parents having some problems."

Marisol nodded as her stupid tears filled her eyes.

"So make the connection between that and you trying to be something you're not, Marisol."

Marisol wrung her hands together as she looked down at her nails painted with clear polish.

"I feel like all of it—the money, our lifestyle, all the nice things—is what caused the problems for my parents," Marisol admitted. "Having my family together is more important to me than stupid clothes, cars and money."

Marisol swiped at the tears that fell from her eyes.

Sasha reached over and squeezed Marisol's wrist comfortingly. "Marisol, please believe me when I tell you that one thing about problems is that they are universal, baby—White, Black, Hispanic, rich, middle-class or poor. It doesn't matter if you dress it up or not. It's all the same and pain hurts the same no matter how much money you got in the bank."

Marisol nodded at the wisdom of her words.

"Plus, Marisol, whatever is happening with your parents is not your cross to bear. You are taking way too much on your shoulders, Marisol. Way too much."

Marisol wiped her tears as she looked over at Mrs. Lester. "It's hard, you know, Mrs. Lester?"

"So why make it worse by not being who you are meant to be, Marisol? And you, Miss Thang, are definitely fabulous."

Marisol smiled. "I am, right?" she stated more than asked as she snapped her fingers in a round circle in the air before she winked saucily.

"Now *there's* Marisol," Sasha assured her. "Welcome back."

FIERCE FASHIONISTA 15?
Posted in *Uncategorized* on October 4 @ 6:00 a.m. by thedivaofdish
So today is the supposed big day for all you Pace Academy students. Starr Lester's Fierce and Fabulous Fashionista 15 party is tonight. If you didn't get an invite don't kill yourself...because I know someone who did. And I will bring you all the juicy details as they text them to me...right here...all night long.
Smooches,
Pace Academy's Diva of Dish

210 comments

thirty-four

Starr
October 4 @ 8:00 p.m. | Mood: Excited

starr was nervous, more nervous than she had ever been in her whole life.

Still, with one camera in her face 24/7 she maintained a cool facade, ignoring the sounds of preparations from the models, makeup and hair people hustling and bustling around her.

Thankfully she was like a bride on her wedding day— ready to turn it all over to her event planner, Kyra Stone. She had done all her planning, running, ducking and dodging—even handled posing with her parents and a bunch of celebrities on the hot-pink carpet outside the mansion. All she wanted to do was enjoy herself and party…well, like it was her birthday party. LOL.

So calm down, Starr, she reminded herself as she fanned herself with her hands behind the curtain at the rear of the stage. The last thing she wanted to do was ruin her makeup by Sam Fine and her hair by Kimberly Kimble. Starr walked on her four-inch Louis V gladiator sandals to inspect her dramatic makeup and new do. She loved them both—especially the longer tracks of hair added to her bangs to give her an edgier flipped-up do that was so Rihanna.

Her black-sequin one-shoulder Gucci dress was perfect. The addition of a wide belt and sequined leggings gave it just the edge she wanted. Her mother's stylist was the ish for real.

Starr danced a little to the music thumping through the walls as she waited to make her grand entrance.

At the fashion-show dress rehearsal, Starr finally saw the decor of the private mansion they'd rented in New York. It was just what she wanted: pretty and festive all at once in bright vibrant colors with images of the fashion-ista flashing against the walls along with her name in lights.

Starr cracked the curtain open a bit and looked dead in the face of her parents standing at the end of the long runway. That made her feel way better than the four hundred people in attendance at the standing-room-only party.

"You okay, boo?" Kyra asked, coming up to stand beside her with her clipboard and walkie-talkie in hand.

"I'm ready," Starr said.

"You look beautiful," Kyra said. "Remember you have

like four wardrobe changes so be mindful of your time and don't wander too far."

"Got it." Starr gave the camera her winning Starr smile.

"The dancers should be finishing up now." Kyra walked down the steps. "Models, line up. Remember as soon as Starr makes her entrance and the music changes it's a go."

Beep-beep. The walkie-talkie sounded. *"White screen lowering."*

Kyra gave her a reassuring smile as Starr struck her pose knowing the shadow of her image would be visible on the white screen at the end of the stage.

Beep-beep.

"Images of Starr playing."

Beep-beep.

"Starr's a go in five, four, three, two…"

The curtains opened.

Beep-beep.

Play voiceover.

Starr strutted down the runway, aware of the shadow she made, as her voice played over the loudspeakers and sound system to an original beat just for her by one of her father's best producers.

"I am Starr Lester…but you already know that. I am fierce. I am a fashionista. And today I'm celebrating turning fifteen. There's nothing I would rather do than show my swag. I wear many designers, my fashion ideas are unlimited and my style game is infinite."

Starr kicked through the thin white paper and posed again to thunderous applause as her heart beat like crazy.

She took that moment to look out at the sea of people before her all dressed in white. Everyone was here to celebrate with her. Right then she knew she lived up to her name.

Starr applauded along with the rest of the partygoers as the models all did their last walk. Her mother's stylist had really hooked her up and whether they knew it or not, the four hundred people in attendance had just seen a show to rival those during Fashion Week.

The music changed and everyone started dancing, including Starr, Marisol and Dionne. Starr was glad her parents went off to their own VIP room upstairs.

"You two look so cute," she leaned in close to yell to them.

And they did.

Starr was glad her parents talked her out of a date and told her to just enjoy her friends.

Dionne's usually straight hair was a riot of curls and perfectly suited the white leather-and-suede strapless dress she wore with leggings and lots of chunky jewelry.

And Marisol, thank the heavens she had found her inner fabulousness again.

Her hair was pulled up into a loose topknot. The large diamond hoop earrings that she wore, Starr had no doubt were real. Her makeup was perfect with her smoky eyes and nude lip gloss. An all-white halter jumpsuit fit her so perfectly.

DIVAS 4 sure. Ow!

Starr made a mental note to thank her mother for talking to Marisol. If any woman could make someone claim their fabulousness...it was Sasha Lester.

Starr grabbed the girls by the hand so they wouldn't miss one detail of the over-the-top party: candy stations, an appetizer buffet and an ice sculpture of her name. Private rooms were set up with a cigar bar and alcohol for the adults at the party. A swag room filled with goodies for those designated as VIP. And another room was filled with nothing but her gifts. The works.

Starr loved every single minute of it.

Starr was antsy as her mother zipped her up into her fourth and final outfit of the night: a strapless white sequin dress with ostrich feathers around the base—her only white outfit. Her metallic Louboutin gladiator heels set it off perfectly. "Hurry, Ma, I don't want to miss the performers," Starr said excitedly as she held her face up for her makeup to be touched up for the gazillionth time.

"I got you, baby girl," Sasha said, her hair now a glossy auburn and perfectly curled, looking brighter against the strapless jumpsuit she wore with a killer white alligator clutch. "Okay, go ahead."

Dionne and Marisol grabbed her hands and the Pacesetters flew out of the dressing room and toward the stage where Kyra immediately removed the rope to let them up. Starr walked carefully in her heels.

"Here's the birthday girl," her father shouted into the mic as he reached out and took her hand in his.

Starr smiled and pushed her bangs from her eyes.

"Just for you, baby," Cole said. "Y'all ready for the concert?"

"Yeah!" the crowd roared back.

Cole laughed. "Okay, here we go. First up, party people, Lahron the Don!"

Starr whirled and looked at Dionne, who was just as shocked as she was as her father came onto the stage with all his swagger in full effect as his hit "Watch Me" filled the air.

And one after the other some of the top names in the R&B and hip-hop music industry took the stage to perform.

Starr lost count.

All she knew was that she was sweaty and she didn't care.

"And our last performer for the night—with the most important song of all, y'all can help him out. New TopStarr artist, Jordan Jackson."

The curtains opened and her cake rose from the center of the stage as Jordan walked onstage singing "Happy Birthday" and looking far too good to be someone she was mad at. She hardly noticed the pure perfection that was her cake in the shape of several designer handbags and shoes as Jordan stepped up to her and grabbed her hand, dropping to one knee.

Everyone sang along with him, but Starr only heard Jordan. She only saw Jordan.

"Happy Birthday to you-ooh."

Jordan rose to his feet and bent down to press a kiss to her cheek. "Happy birthday, Starr," he whispered into her ear, before sneaking a small kiss on her neck.

Wowzer!

Starr felt her knees give out beneath her as she swooned. She did the unthinkable, the unimaginable, the impossible.

She passed out onstage.

thirty-five

Dionne
October 4 @ 10:45 p.m. | Mood: Sympathetic

"**ohmygod,**" Starr kept saying into the hands covering her face, sounding more like Marisol than herself.

Dionne just stood by helplessly, knowing Starr *had* to be embarrassed, especially since her little leg spread during the fall meant everyone in the front row could see her unmentionables. Needless to say, camera phones went into overdrive at that point.

Starr Lester passing out at her Fierce and Fabulous Fashionista Fifteen party was going to be all over the gossip blogs before morning.

Dionne fought the urge to check the YBF site via her cell phone. "At least you didn't do a Britney and go commando," she said.

Starr dropped her hands just long enough to shoot Dionne an eye dagger.

"Sorry," Dionne mumbled, moving away from Starr as her parents came back into the room with Kyra the event planner and a new woman introduced as Topp-Starr's lead publicist, Anna Lowitz.

Her father dropped down onto the sofa next to her and wrapped his arms around her shoulders. "Watch Anna make her money, baby girl," he assured her.

"Okay, people, here's the story. Stick to it," Anna assured them with a smile that was an odd mix of wickedness and niceness all at once.

Dionne was heading from the ladies' room when Reggie suddenly stepped into her path. "Hey you," she said, caught off guard by his sudden appearance. "You look nice."

And he did in his all-white dress shirt, vest and linen pants with a fresh pair of Air Force 1s.

"You, too." Reggie reached out and grabbed her hand.

Dionne frowned a little as she pulled her hand away gently. "I got to get back to Starr," she told him.

"How is she?"

"Much better. Thanks."

Dionne eased past him.

"Hey, Dionne, I thought we was hollerin' or whatever," he said, licking his lips as she turned to face him.

As the sounds of old-school Big Daddy Kane filled the air, Dionne crossed her arms over her chest as she eyed him. "You want the truth?" she asked him.

"The whole horny-vibe thing you're giving off is a turnoff because I'm not giving up the goodies to you or anybody else," she told him with the kind of confidence that would make her mama proud.

Reggie reached up and smoothed his skinny hand over his fade. "I really like you, Dionne," he admitted. "For real."

Dionne leaned back against the wall as she tilted her head to look at him. "Then start fresh. Come correct. Tighten up your game. Trust and believe I am not your ordinary Pace Academy girl. I've seen things some of these bourgie girls will *never* see," she told him, surprised by her own honesty. "If you want to talk to me then cut the crap."

Reggie tossed his head back and laughed. "Dang, you straight up, huh?"

Dionne nodded. "Pretty much all day. Every day."

"Okay, then let's start over," he said, holding out his hand. "I'm Reggie."

After a slight pause she slid her hand into his. "I'm Dionne," she told him, with a soft smile.

"Excuse me, everyone. Please make your way out to the backyard," came the announcement over the loud-speaker.

Dionne gave Reggie another smile. "I gotta go," she told him, before turning and quickly making her way through the massive crowd of people to the VIP area.

"Gift time," Starr said as she grabbed Dionne and Marisol's hands and pulled them behind her as she followed the bodyguards clearing a path for them and her camera crew through the people.

But what do you give a little girl who already has everything? Dionne wondered.

The cool October air felt good against their skin as the Pacesetters came to a stop next to Starr's parents. Dionne smiled as Starr fidgeted in her Louboutins. She was so ready for her present.

"Happy birthday, Starr!"

The colorful lights and explosion of fireworks filled the sky. The entire crowd of people oohed and aahed at the spectacle.

With her head tilted to the sky, Dionne wished Hassan was there with her. Getting over him wasn't as easy as she thought it would be.

"Look, star-shaped fireworks," someone exclaimed.

As the fireworks came to an end, Dionne looked around at the still-upturned faces of the partygoers. She smiled as Starr's father—looking fine in his white-on-white tux—grabbed his wife around the waist and kissed her.

"Honk-honk!"

Everyone turned at the sound of the car horn. A collective gasp raced through the crowd as the fireworks were completely forgotten.

Starr let out a high-pitched squeal of excitement. "Ohmygod, Ilovemyparents. Ohmygod, Ilovemyparents. Ohmygod, ILOVEMYPARENTS!!!"

Pulling up to a stop on the rear driveway was a brand-new gleaming Range Rover HSE in a light sand color with twenty-two-inch rims. The interior was customized in khaki or sand with hot-pink trim complete with her name and little star symbols in the headrests. Marcus stepped out of the Range Rover to stand beside it in his black-on-black uniform.

Starr hugged her parents quickly before she rushed over to her gift.

As the crowd surrounded Starr and the car, Dionne fell back a bit. She really had to stop a moment to take it all in. She went from 16th Avenue in Newark to hanging out with famous people at private parties at mansions in New York.

She grinned.

Life *was* pretty fa-bu-lous.

thirty-six

Marisol
October 5 @ 2:00 a.m. | Mood: Reflective

there was no sleeping for the Pacesetters. They all were still excited from the party and wide-awake even though they hadn't slept. They lounged in their colorful pajamas on the floor in the center of Starr's room. The music was pumping from Starr's surround sound system. They had glass bowls of their favorite snacks on the floor between them.

Marisol was reading a book—since she was abstaining from using her laptop.

Dionne was loading pictures of the party onto her Facebook page.

Starr was revising her list of things to go over with her party planner for the brunch tomorrow. "My mom said the publicist is trying to squeeze some of the party photos on *Essence*'s site," Starr said.

Marisol looked over at Dionne and then at a very bored-looking Starr. "I didn't notice a photographer."

"And thus our instructions for them to stay out of sight were heeded," Starr drawled.

Dionne laughed as Marisol tossed a small star-shaped pillow at her friend.

"Does your dad's publicist get photo approval?" Dionne asked.

Starr looked at Dionne with a surprised expression. "Dang, you're a quick learner, girl," she said with a smile.

Now it was Dionne's turn to toss a pillow.

Marisol had to duck to avoid having it hit the top of her head.

Starr caught it with ease. Of course. "She has a friend that works at the magazine and she's going to tell us for sure tomorrow."

Marisol shrugged, forcing herself not to care as she closed the book. "The sleepover in the pool house was fun but this is better," she said, changing the subject.

"Yeah, we couldn't talk ourselves to sleep like we normally do," Starr said as she put down her glittery notepad and fuzzy-topped pencil.

Dionne looked up from her laptop. "Some of the girls were watching us so hard. Thank God we didn't miss and fart or something."

The girls all giggled.

"That's all a part of being a Pacesetter," Starr reminded them. "In life you either lead or you follow. I'd much rather be a leader than a follower."

"And there are plenty of lost souls who need someone to follow," Dionne drawled as she typed something on her computer. "Style and swagger ain't nothin' to play with."

"Ooh, did y'all see the white jumpsuit Inez had on… with a red thong!" Starr frowned and shivered at the thought.

"That was nothing compared to Kimmie's sweating in her white jeans," Dionne added.

Marisol just eyed them both.

"Well, I heard that some of the boys tried to sneak into the cigar room," Dionne said.

"They're stupid. Nothing but old men smoke cigars," Marisol said with a frown.

"Okay," Dionne agreed before she grabbed her brush and worked the tangles from her hair.

Marisol looked up when Starr nudged her with her foot. Starr winked at her and then nudged her chin up in Dionne's direction.

"Well, I also heard that some girl was spotted by the bathroom with Reggie," Starr said slyly.

Dionne's head shot up and her eyes were wide. "Who?" she asked with much too much attitude.

"Wow, someone is sounding big-time jealous," Starr teased.

"*That's* a big nothing," Dionne said.

"You didn't kiss him, did you?" Marisol asked with a frown as she reached into the large bowl of jelly beans on the floor.

Dionne shook her head.

"Good, because he's probably a playa anyway. All boys are," Marisol said firmly.

She didn't miss the way Starr and Dionne exchanged a long look.

"I was putting his little horny self in check always tryna be fresh on the low like I'm DumbDumbDaDa and don't know what he means."

"Well, he's a cutie," Starr assured her.

"Trust me, I know that and so does he."

The girls laughed and gave each other some dap.

Marisol fell quiet as Starr and Dionne continued to go through the ever-changing list of Pace Academy Hot Boyz. Marisol wasn't at all in the mood for crushes. She rose to her feet and walked over to the closed patio doors.

She'd reclaimed her fabulosity but would she ever reclaim her happiness? The weight of her parents' marriage was on her shoulders.

"Marisol! Who looks better, Souljah Boy or Sammie?" Dionne asked.

"They're both cute," Marisol said, turning away from the patio doors.

"No, you have to pick," Starr stressed, as she took the brush from Dionne and attacked her hair, sculpting it to her head before she tied it down with her silk hair scarf.

"Okay, Sammie," Marisol said as she slowly walked back over to reclaim her spot on the floor. "I like his style better. Souljah Boy's killing me softly with those shades and military shirts all the time."

"Oooh, I co-sign that one," Starr agreed.

"Okay, Starr, Bow Wow or Omarion?" Dionne asked, shifting her laptop from her lap to the floor.

Starr tapped the hairbrush against the palm of her hand. "Well, both are my boys…but I say, Omarion. And you two better not tell them I said that," she warned as she pointed the end of the brush at both of them.

Marisol gathered her hair up in her hands and then quickly twisted it into a topknot as she laughed and continued to play Who Looks Better. Being away from her parents, she could almost get lost in the girls' frivolous talk about boys and forget the tension and unrest between her parents. Almost.

thirty-seven

Starr
October 5 @ 10:00 a.m. | Mood: Thankful

starr had been the first one up at eight o'clock thanks
to her vibrating cell phone alarm clock she held in her
hand. Since they hadn't gone to sleep until 3:00 a.m., she
figured she would make up for it after the brunch—the
finale to her Fierce and Fabulous Fashionista Fifteen
weekend. Starr allowed herself a little leisurely "pamper
me" time before she exited her spa bathroom to find her
mom sitting on her bed talking to Marisol and Dionne.

"Morning, birthday girl," Sasha sang in her famous
raspy voice that had earned her legions of fans.

Starr smiled as her mother stood and held her close to
her chest, rocking her back and forth. She allowed herself
to enjoy the moment, reminding her of when she was just
a toddler and her parents would hug and kiss her like they
couldn't get enough. "Thanks, Ma," Starr said.

"You're welcome," Sasha said, patting Starr's back before she released her. "You girls get dressed. Everyone should be arriving in a couple of hours and your camera crew is already here. Oh, and so is the makeup artist."

That made the Pacesetters all jump to attention and scurry to their feet. Sasha laughed.

"I got dibs on the bathroom next," Dionne called out.

"No, I do," Marisol asserted.

"Starr, throw on a robe and go get your hair and makeup done. They're setting up in the game room," Sasha said over her shoulder before she left the room.

Starr did just that, thinking it was so hilarious for Marisol and Dionne to argue over a bathroom in a house with at least six bathrooms. She was headed down the stairs when she looked out the large window over the second-story landing and spotted Jordan's car slowly pulling up the brick-paved driveway.

Starr paused as her heart pounded at the very thought of her ex-crush. Would she ever get over him? Would he release his claim on her heart?

"Hey, there's my Starr."

She turned and watched as her father jogged down the stairs, already dressed in a linen camp shirt and jeans with all his jewelry and swag in place even this early in the morning. "Hi, Daddy."

He paused next to her on the stairs. "Oh, Jordan's here."

Starr didn't miss the sideward glance he gave her. "Yeah, I see."

Cole Lester wrapped his arm around Starr's shoulder and pulled her close to him to plant a kiss to the side of her head. "Did you like your surprise last night?" he asked.

Starr's entire body went warm as she thought of how that surprise had caused her to faint. "He did okay," she said lamely.

"Okay?" Cole balked.

Starr just shrugged as she looked up at her father.

"Okay, I know what. Let's just stay in our lanes. Shopping and partying?"

Starr smiled. "I got it. Making hit music?"

"I'm all over it."

They bumped fists before her father jogged down the stairs alone. Starr purposefully waited, taking a seat on the upholstered chaise under the window because she didn't want to bump into Jordan on his way to her father's studio.

When she did finally venture down the stairs, she still had Jordan on her mind. All of her plans for them to be *the power couple* at Pace were ruined because Heather was serving it up like hotcakes.

No rides to school with her boo. (She had already decided that Jordan looked like a boo.)

No rolling up to the upcoming formal together—where they would have been named King and Queen of The Ball—of course. No cutesy couple nicknames like Tomkat, Brangelina. They could've been Starrdan or Jorstarr or something like that.

Starr pushed aside all her silly thoughts.

There was no need crying or dwelling over spilled milk.

Starr was enjoying the brunch just as much as her party last night. She took a sip of her nonalcoholic mimosa as she surveyed everything in the huge white tent on the west lawn of their estate. The tent had been completely transformed with a dozen round tables, flower centerpieces, draped silk and glittering chandeliers. The buffet of eggs, sausages, bacon, fruits, pastries, pancakes and miniature quiches was as appetizing to the eye as it was filling. Everyone who was invited attended and fully complied with Starr's dress code of "pretend you're going to church." Three long tables held all of her birthday gifts that she still had yet to open—well, almost all. The present from Jordan was unopened and buried deep in her closet.

Starr had no plans to open it, but she didn't quite have the nerve to send it back to him either.

"Oh, my God, this seafood quiche is sooo good," Dionne said as she took another mouthful.

"Well, how about you get that little tidbit off your chin because the cameras are pointed this way," Starr told her.

She smiled as Dionne whirled in her seat, turning her back to the camera.

Starr had a good time but she had to admit that she was tired and ready for the weekend to come to an end. She sought and found the eye of her party planner, giving her the cue to wrap up the brunch.

Starr accepted the cordless microphone that someone handed to her and rose to her feet. Moments later the waitstaff wheeled in carts laden with silver-wrapped gift boxes. With her hair in a jazzy curly hairdo, her makeup flawless and her strapless ballerina-styled dress she didn't feel a bit of nervousness having all eyes on her…until she spotted her father and Jordan headed across the lawn toward the tent.

Starr quickly turned away so that they were out of her line of vision. "I just wanted to thank you all for coming out this weekend—especially those of you here who are my VIPs—and celebrating my Fierce and Fabulous Fifteen with me. As a token of my thanks, here's a little sum'n sum'n for you all to remember a weekend I know I will *never* forget."

Even Dionne and Marisol were surprised as they were handed gift boxes.

"What's this?" Dionne mouthed to her with a curious expression.

When one of the staff handed Jordan one she started to storm across the room and snatch it from his "been all on Heather" hands but she forced a stiff, fake smile instead.

Everyone oohed and aahed at the netbooks.

"Each one has been preloaded with a video documenting the entire weekend and only those of you here are getting one," Starr told them.

Starr looked around as everyone played with their new gadget. She was glad the videographer was able to stay up all night editing so that it was ready for today. She was sure her father's wallet had a lot to do with it. And it was worth it as everyone swarmed around her to offer their thanks.

Starr reveled in the spotlight.

She was a Starr after all.

thirty-eight

Marisol
October 5 @ 4:00 p.m. | Mood: Completely Confused

Marisol was exhausted by the time her driver pulled up in front of their Saddle River estate. She grabbed her tote, slid on her shades and climbed out the back of the silver Jaguar. Her driver set her Louis Vuitton suitcase beside her.

"Enjoy the rest of your day, Miss Rivera," he said, before walking back to climb into the driver's seat of the Jaguar.

Marisol pulled the handle of her suitcase up and pulled it behind her as she climbed the steps to their minimansion.

"Hello, Miss Rivera," Porton the gardener greeted her as she walked past.

"Hello, Porton."

Once she entered the house, she felt like she could finally get some sleep.

"I'm home," she hollered as soon as she closed the front door.

She smiled at the two maids dusting the foyer as she left her suitcase and went in search of her parents.

"Just the girl I want to see."

Marisol turned, surprised to see her mother walking out of the kitchen behind her. "Come," she beckoned Marisol, taking her daughter's hand to wrap around her arms as she led her into the atrium off the living room.

"I've missed you, Marisol. You had a good time at Starr's?" Yasmine asked in Spanish.

"It was a lot of fun."

"And did she like the charm bracelet you gave her?" Yasmine asked as they sat down on the black wrought-iron furniture surrounded by the beauty of the flowers and the plants.

Marisol nodded, instead of explaining Starr's custom of opening her gifts alone.

Yasmine flipped her hair over her shoulder as she lightly patted her daughter's hand. "Okay, so, Sasha called me," she said, reverting to her slightly broken English.

Marisol's eyes widened.

"I wanted to talk to you about that and first let me apologize for not keeping you out of this." Yasmine's eyes were filled with love as she looked at her daughter. "I had no idea that you knew of our troubles."

Marisol looked away but her mother lightly touched her chin and turned her head back.

"Next I want to assure you that I love your father

very much and I know he loves me, as well. We are not getting a divorce and we will get through this and come out even better."

Marisol frowned in confusion.

Was it true?

Was it not true?

Did her mother forgive him?

Did he deserve to be forgiven?

What the...?

"In time everything will go back to normal. But for now there is nothing you did wrong and there is no reason for you to let our burdens weigh you down."

Marisol had so many questions, but she held them. From a young age, the Rivera children had been taught to respect their elders and she wouldn't dare think of questioning her mother. No matter how confused she was.

So it was okay for her father to cheat?

Marisol frowned as her mother hugged her close to her chest.

Her mother said everything was going back to normal, but the question was—when? And even more—why?

NOBODY BROUGHT ME BAD NEWS!!!
Posted in Good Gossip on October 6 @ 1:00 p.m. by thedivaofdish

So everyone had a ball at Starr's party this weekend. Big whoop-de-doo. That's right, no one had anything bad to say. My spies said they had a good time. Guess all that free swag she gave out bought their loyalty. Of course, getting another gas-guzzling, environment-hating SUV is soooo irresponsible, but of course to be fabulous is always like...whateva. *side eye*

Of course we all heard about Starr passing out onstage and even giggled (or laughed hysterically in my case) at the idea of it—until we heard that she has some illness. I have way too big a heart to joke about something like that or post the pictures that flooded my inbox.

In other news, heard Marisol Rivera was back to her old ways. Dang, I thought we had a convert. Starr probably wouldn't let her in unless she played dress-up. LOL.
Smooches,
Pace Academy's Diva of Dish

55 comments

thirty-nine

Dionne
October 6 @ 4:25 p.m. | Mood: Loving

DIONNE took a huge bite of her Mrs. Field's white chunk and macadamia cookie as she walked alongside her mom in Livingston Mall. "That's cute," she said around a mouthful, pointing to a pair of shoes in the Nine West window display.

Risha's earrings hit against each other as she turned her head to look where her daughter pointed. "Do you ever wish I could buy you all those expensive things like your daddy?" she asked.

"Nine West? That's not expensive," she quipped, bumping her thin shoulder against her mother's. "But I know what you mean. I'm not crazy, Ma."

"Neither am I. Answer me," she pressed.

Dionne wiped her hands in a napkin. "Well, I don't understand why you won't take money from Daddy," she said simply, tossing her napkin and now-empty cookie bag into the trash. "We could move to a better house in a better neighborhood. And you could buy yourself some of those nice things. You deserve it, Ma."

Risha sighed as she sat down on a wooden bench outside Victoria's Secret. "First off, I work every day. And if I want to buy me a hundred-dollar bag I can—"

"Uhm, Ma, most of those bags are like five hundred dollars or more," Dionne told her. "Starr just got a Ricky bag that was twenty thousand dollars."

Risha arched an eyebrow before she fanned herself. Her mother always fanned when she was confronted with foolishness. "My point is...that I can take care of myself. The only thing I want your father to do is take care of you and I have to admit that he does that."

Dionne nodded, wishing her mother wasn't so independent. "But he wants to pay you child support. He wants to give you a house in a better neighborhood."

Risha shook her head. "And what's wrong with our neighborhood... It's not like your daddy's, right?"

"Well..."

Risha laughed as she nudged Dionne with her knee. "You know your father has asked me a few times to let you live with him since I won't take the money."

Dionne tensed as she waited for whatever was coming next.

"I'm not crazy. I understand that it can't be easy for you going between my world and his—especially with his being so *fabulous*," she said, jokingly mocking her daughter.

Dionne could see that her mother was hurt and that hurt her deeply. "Ma—"

Risha held up her hand. "No, let me finish. I'm not saying yes but I'm not saying no anymore. I'm saying that I will think about it…if it's what you want."

Dionne did a major pause. A full-time life of luxury with her dad or staying at home with her Moms? It was like her dreams were being offered to her on a silver platter. So why didn't she jump at the opportunity? Why didn't she run her mouth and push her mother onto her side when she was so obviously on the edge?

Why did a tiny piece of her feel like her mother didn't want her around anymore?

"Is that what you want, Dionne?" her mother asked again. "Do you want to go live with your father?"

Dionne wished in a big-time way that she had a cookie to shove in her mouth because she wasn't ready to answer. Not yet.

Dionne was sitting on the front stoop listening to her iPod and hoping Hassan would come and see her. She missed him.

Ding.

Picture mail, she thought as she used her thumb to open the text.

"No, he didn't!" Dionne laughed at the picture of her dancing with Reggie in the center of the crowd at the party. Beneath the photo it read:

CUTE COUPLE, RIGHT?

She shook her head as she texted him back:

DIVADIDI: MAYBE 1 DAY
BIG REG: 1 DAY SOON, LIL MA. 1 DAY SOON.
BIG REG: I'M GONE CALL U LATER.
DIVADIDI: K.

Dionne just put her phone down on the stoop as the sounds of Keyshia Cole filled her earbuds. The music made her think of Hassan—definitely not Reggie.

Reggie's money and looks just didn't compare. No boy made her feel the way Hassan did.

"Grandma was right," Dionne muttered as she dropped her head down and looked at her iPod. "You never miss your water till your well runs dry."

Dionne looked up at the park and frowned at the sight of a teenage couple walking and holding hands. "I bet Hassan likes to hold hands and walk," she said, sounding dejected and down. Big-time.

She called his cell phone and after one ring it went to voicemail. More like was sent straight to voice mail.

"If it ain't Miss Bourgie slummin'."

Dionne looked up from her phone to find Joshia and Kim walking toward her. She hated that their friendship had come to this because the three of them had been so close. But was it her fault her daddy made a hit record? They flipped on her.

She slid her phone into the back pocket of her jeans as she eyed them as they walked by her stoop.

"Hoping you wasn't calling Hassan because Jalisha got

him on lockdown right now, boo-boo," Joshia said over her shoulder.

"Oops!" Kim laughed. "How sad, too bad for you."

Dionne's heart sank at their gossip but she didn't quit staring back until they had turned the corner. Hassan and Jalisha—she was the hood version of Heather. Heck, no.

Is that why he sent her call to voice mail?

"Oh, no, he didn't!" Dionne hopped to her feet, leaving the porch to head down the street. Hassan lived in the big apartment building on the corner of 18th Avenue and 18th Street—just two blocks over.

The streetlights came on as the sun started to set. Dionne was halfway there when she thought about turning back. Once she turned the corner on 18th Avenue she wished she had.

Hassan was sitting on the front stoop of his building with some thick, red-boned girl sitting on the step beneath him…between his legs.

Dionne stood there on that corner and felt like her heart broke into a thousand pieces, especially when Hassan dipped his head and pressed a quick kiss to Jalisha's big, juicy, wet-looking mouth.

Her breath probably stinks like Puffed Cheez Doodles, Dionne thought, knowing she was acting like a grade-school kid.

Turning around, Dionne walked head-on into a solid chest. "Excuse me," she said, stepping past them to quickly walk away.

Reggie was looking a lot more appealing right now, she

thought as she shoved her hands into the pockets of her leather motorcycle jacket.

"Yo, give it up, Ma."

Dionne stopped and looked sideways. A tall skinny dude in a hoodie walked up onto the sidewalk beside her—a stick-up kid. (Side note to God: What in the world did I do 2 deserve this?)

Dionne's heart beat like crazy as she started taking off the big bamboo gold earrings she wore. *And I love my throwback doorknockers, too,* she thought as he snatched them from her hand.

"iPod and bracelets, too," he demanded, his face masked by the darkness of the hood.

Her gifts from Starr and Marisol! Okay, she loved them. She hated to part with them like this, but she wasn't trying to die for them.

She handed over the iPod and then removed each of the bracelets: *LOVE, FAITH, PEACE* and *STRENGTH.*

Humph, I need those mugs more than ever right now.

"Matter of fact my girl gone like that jack. Run that, too."

"Ain't this 'bout a bunch of bull," Dionne muttered as she unzipped it.

"Ain't it," he had the nerve to joke with a laugh before he snatched the coat from her hand, and ran across the street to hop up the stone wall like a dang-on frog before the darkness of the park cloaked him.

Dionne ran home, not caring that she probably looked crazy.

She didn't stop running until she was banging on the front door of their apartment. As soon as her Moms opened the door, Dionne fell into her arms. "I got robbed, Ma."

Risha rushed to close and lock the front door as she held Dionne with one hand. "What happened?"

"I got robbed!" Dionne wailed as she dropped down onto the sofa.

Risha grabbed the phone and called the police. "They're on the way, baby," her mother said. "You okay?"

Dionne nodded as she laid her head in her mama's lap. "They just made me take off all my jewelry and my coat."

Risha stroked the length of Dionne's hair. "You think it was somebody that knew who your daddy was?"

"I don't know. I don't think so."

"We need to call your daddy," Risha said, reaching for the phone to quickly dial him.

Dionne wished they didn't, because she knew he was going to flip out.

"Lahron, hey, this Risha. Listen, Dionne just got robbed." Risha winced and held the phone from her head.

Dionne was right.

"She's fine. We're waiting on the police."

Dionne closed her eyes at the sound of her father's voice echoing through the phone line—but then when she closed her eyes she clearly envisioned Hassan and that girl.

Between them and the robbery, Dionne was sure she had just experienced the worst night of her life.

After the police came and left, Dionne sat on the sofa and waited for the fireworks to kick off.

"This never would have happened if you moved out this neighborhood like I told you, Risha, or you let her live with me," Lahron told her, his bodyguard standing by the door looking like he was waiting for a chance to break someone—anyone—in two pieces.

"You're right," Risha admitted softly, wiping her face with her hands.

Dionne looked at her mother in shock.

"You can't always be right, Risha." Lahron stopped and then swung around to look at her. "What did you say?"

"Dionne and I were just talking about her living with you and I told her I would think about it...and this mess happens," Risha sighed. "Maybe it's a sign."

Dionne's head swung from left and then to right as she eyed her parents. She felt like her life was moving in slow motion as her parents started discussing the who, what, when, where and why of her moving in with her daddy.

Dionne eyed her mama. How could she bounce to the lap of luxury and leave her mama behind her? Even though she prayed for this day like her grandmama prayed for winning the lottery, Dionne felt panicked. "No!"

Lahron and Risha looked down at her.

Dionne jumped to her feet. "I'm not going. I'm not leaving my mother."

Risha frowned. "First off, watch your tone, Dionne."

*Okay, Mama **never** play.* "Sorry."

"Second, I love you, little girl." Risha pulled Dionne to her feet and hugged her close. "But this might be for the best."

"Do we have to decide tonight?" Dionne asked, wanting time of her own to think it through.

Lahron shoved his hands into the front pockets of his distressed jeans. "Risha, let me holler at you in private," he said, nudging his head toward her bedroom.

Dionne watched as her parents disappeared in the room. *Now a really big solution would be for them to start kicking it again,* she thought, knowing that it truly was wishful thinking.

Sighing, she looked down at her bare wrist, wishing she had her bracelets to play with. How was she going to explain that to Starr and Dionne? *Oh, I was walking home in Newark—you know, the place where I live but you guys don't know it—and a stick-up kid got me.*

Obviously that was not going to work.

Hopefully they won't notice while I think of something to tell them.

Or maybe I can just ask Daddy to buy me a new set?

Sighing, Dionne tucked her legs underneath her on the sofa. She felt anxious and jittery from the robbery... and from seeing Hassan with another girl. Needing a distraction, Dionne reached for the remote and turned on the TV.

She was flipping through the channels when her mother's bedroom door opened. Dionne put the TV on mute, silencing a Jordan Sparks video.

"Okay, Dionne, your father is going to buy *you* a nice small house—"

Dionne screamed before she rushed off the couch and squeezed her daddy with her arms and then shifted over to hug her mama hard. "Thank you, Mama," she told her, because Dionne knew how hard this was for her.

Dionne started doing a dance.

"The house has to be something you can buy so that the deed goes in a trust for Dionne until she is twenty-one. I'm not moving to no white neighborhood—there are plenty of decent black neighborhoods. I will be paying rent because I'm not having anybody try and run my home. And lastly, I'm not moving too far from my job."

Dionne didn't care if her mother had a thousand more stipulations. They were moving and maybe, just maybe, a little bit of her fabulous life with her daddy could merge with her normal life with her mom.

forty

Marisol
October 6 @ 6:00 a.m. | Mood: Rejuvenated

"**GOOD** *morning, Marisol. Rise and shine. Today is the first day of the rest of your fabulous life.*"

Marisol grunted softly as she rolled over on the Egyptian cotton sheets on her bed. With a long stretch and a yawn she reached over to her nightstand and turned her alarm clock off.

She flipped the covers back before she hopped to her bare feet. She was getting up extra early. She had a lot of catching up to do.

Marisol headed straight to her adjoining bathroom and began going through her prestrike morning ritual. When she emerged forty-five minutes later, she felt more like herself than ever.

Hair: freshly shampooed, conditioned, dried and then

straightened with a ceramic flat iron in a glossy side ponytail.

Face: a minifacial left her feeling tingly beneath the light moisturizer she wore with just very light mascara, a light dusting of blush and sheer lip gloss.

Body: soaked and scrubbed in a milk bath that left her light brown skin soft.

Marisol turned on her iPod docking station and the sounds of Beyoncé filled the air. With nothing but a plush towel wrapped around her, she danced over to her walk-in closet.

"'Standing in the light of your halo, I got my angel now...'" Marisol said as she tried to mimick the lyrics. She was Beyoncé's off-key backup singer. She rushed to get dressed in her perfectly coordinated Ralph Lauren outfit.

Once she was dressed, Marisol stepped onto the pedestal in front of the three-way mirror. She smiled and posed.

Mrs. Lester was right. The real Marisol was all about the hair, the makeup and the clothes. Always had been, always would be.

The cream silk blouse opened just enough to show a hint of the gold chains she wore—a perfect complement to the stiff cotton gaucho pants she wore with a braided leather belt and the "it" accessory of the season, the Louis V Spicy sandal. Beyoncé, Christina Milian and Ciara all rocked them—which made them a must-have.

She walked to her round dressing table and opened the suede jewelry box to pull out a huge turquoise ring to wear on her index finger and her diamond Rolex.

Right or wrong, Marisol felt like some of her power was back.

Why deny herself?

She would just have to find another way to come to grips with her family drama.

Grabbing her olive-colored alligator leather jacket and her classic Gucci tote, Marisol left her room more than ready for the start of a brand-new fabulous day.

Marisol strutted down the hall, but she backed up a few paces at the sight of her brother's room through his open door.

"You're gross," she told him, holding her nose to block the offending smell of feet, dirty boxers...and... food? *What the...?*

She never could wrap her mind around her parents allowing him to keep his room like that.

Carlos eyed her as he dug in his nose with his index finger and pulled out a huge booger. "Hungry?" he said, as he stood up with his loaded finger pointed dead at her.

Marisol's eyes widened. "You better not," she warned him in rapid Spanish.

He ran at her.

Marisol shrieked and ran. When she almost slid down the length of the hall in her heels, she froze and whirled on him. He pulled up short in surprise. Marisol pointed a manicured finger at him. "If you put that thing on me I will order the maids to clean your room and to throw away all of that creepy, gross crap you keep in that closet," she warned him with the evil eye.

Carlos took a step forward.

"And I'll tell Papi you were the one who used his suede Bruno Maglis as boats for your stupid turtles."

Carlos frowned in thought.

"Or that you gave Mama's new bracelet to that teacher you had a crush on. You know the teacher who kept the bracelet."

Carlos stomped his foot in frustration before he promptly sucked the booger on his finger.

Marisol's stomach went in reverse as she gagged.

He turned and walked back into his room.

Marisol straightened her outfit and smoothed her hair before she turned and continued down the hall. She actually felt herself smile. At least things were starting to feel like normal.

Steadying herself in the heels that were testing her ankles, Marisol held the banister as she made her way down the stairs and into the dining room. She paused in the doorway to see her parents sitting at the table together. Her mother buttered a piece of toast before sitting it on her father's plate. He used the silver decanter to fill his cup with coffee before leaning forward a bit to fill her mother's cup.

No words were said but something in the way they did those small things for each other made Marisol breathe a little bit easier. Like maybe they were going to be okay as a family.

"*Hola, mi familia,*" she said, taking her seat next to her mother at the round table.

"Marisol, you look very pretty. I see you're back to

your old self," Yasmine said, before signaling the maid to bring in the breakfast.

"Just a little something I threw on," she joked before taking a sip of her freshly squeezed orange juice.

She felt her father's eyes on her but he said nothing. The distance between them remained.

"Marisol, where is Carlos? He's going to miss breakfast."

"He's already eaten," Marisol drawled sarcastically as the maid set a plate of bacon, scrambled eggs and French toast before her. She removed the bacon. Now that she was back to being fine and fabulous she had to make sure her bottom half didn't outrace her top half too much.

"Well, I have some good news," Alex said as he cut into his French toast. "My publicist called and *Latina* magazine wants to do an article on your mother."

Yasmine dropped her fork in surprise. "Me?" she said.

"It's up to you, of course," he said with a smile.

"*¡Dios mío! ¡Dios mío! ¡Dios mío!*" Yasmine repeated.

That made Marisol smile.

Yasmine rose from her chair as if to hug Alex but then stopped and sat back down, pressing her hands into her lap and she just offered him a reserved smile. "I'll have to think about it."

That made Marisol's smile fall a bit.

Just like that the tension returned.

Anxious to be on her way, Marisol finished her breakfast and rose to her feet. She bent down to press a kiss to her mother's high cheekbone…and then her father's after a little pause.

He smiled up at her and Marisol had to admit that it felt good to know that something so simple from her could make him happy. Not money. Not the flashing bulbs of the paparazzi. Not the screams of his adoring fans.

Just a kiss from his little girl.

Marisol checked her appearance one last time in her mirror before she climbed out of the back of the Jaguar to join Dionne and Starr. "Whassup, ladies?"

"Nice accessories," Starr said, circling her.

"Good color against your skin," Dionne added.

"Those shoes *are* the bizness."

"Just the right amount of makeup," Dionne said. "Just enough to bring life to your face—"

"And not too much to make you look like a geisha," Starr drawled.

Marisol struck a pose playfully before bursting into a fit of giggles. "Think everyone is ready for all this fabulousness?"

"I know I am," Starr assured her, looking good herself in a black SoCal utility jacket, silk white tank, black skinny jeans and bright red booties.

Dionne was more laid-back in her orange V-neck silk sweaterdress with brown riding boots and a big chunky leather belt.

Marisol saw Jordan when he parked and hopped out of his Mercedes-Benz in all black. She bumped Starr.

"Jordan looks nice," she said, cutting her eye at Dionne before they both cut their eye at Starr. "Did you two plan the whole color-coordination thing?"

"Maybe that's what he whispered in her ear that made her faint?" Dionne teased.

Starr stiffened as she eyed Dionne like rain on a new pair of Louboutin suede shoes. "We swore never to mention that again," she reminded them.

"The kiss on your neck or the fainting?" Marisol asked, biting her lip to keep from giggling.

"With friends like you two, who needs enemies?" Starr snapped, her eyes blazing as she flipped her longer bangs back behind her diamond-studded ear.

Dionne shrugged.

Marisol busied herself reapplying her Cotton Candy lip gloss—it looked and tasted good. As they made their way up the steps and into the building, Marisol could feel the Pace Academy students buzzing with her triumphant return to the spotlight. She felt like a model—no, a supermodel—on the runway. Rihanna onstage. Miss America taking her victory walk with the crown secure on her head. Her father in the center of the baseball field after he'd pitched a no-hitter.

"All eyes on me."

She liked it. She liked it a lot.

Eat that, Diva of Drama.

By the time lunch came around, Marisol had officially reclaimed her spot as a real Pacesetter.

Ding.

UR#1STARR: Hurry up 2 caf.

Marisol's fingers flew off the keyboard.

MARIMARI: ON THE WAY. HEELS HIGHER THAN I THOUGHT.

Marisol closed her locker and locked it, fighting the urge to put on her Juicy Couture sneakers and completely ruin "the look."

"Hi, Marisol."

She paused and looked over her shoulder. She frowned at Percy Gambling standing there. His father was a quarterback with one of the NFL teams and he was completely dominating their division. Percy was a junior. Quite popular for a jock. And the girls all adored him. He was cute in that deep chocolate, dimpled sort of way.

They had done a page on him in their Hot Boyz playbook two summers ago:

Name: Percy "Good to the Last Drop" Gambling
Age: 15
B-Day: 11/24
Fab Cred: Son of Hall of Fame quarterback. Future NBA Top 10 draft pick. Heard he has his parents' guesthouse all to himself. Throws the BEST parties at the guesthouse.
Cute Factor: 8 (The one-dimple thing is weird.)

Style Factor: 10 (Can def show these other lames how 2 do it up! Ow!)
Hot Boyz Rank: #3

What does he want?

"Hi, Percy," she said, her stomach suddenly filled with nerves. Before she did or said something stupid, Marisol turned to continue her journey to the dining hall.

"Hey, hold up," he hollered behind her.

Ohmygod, she thought as she nervously bit the Cotton Candy from her lips. She sighed as she turned again to face him jogging up to her in a preppy Tommy Hilfiger look that he made edgy with a rock-star-style belt and aviator shades.

Okay, can anyone say…yummy?

"I thought I could get your number and call you sometime?" he said, smiling down at her from his six-two frame towering over her barely five-seven self—in heels, mind you. She felt like a dwarf facing him.

Marisol smiled at him and twirled her ponytail around her finger. "Uhm…no. Thanks but no thanks," she told him, before turning and hightailing it away, careful not to trip, slide or stumble as she pressed her heels against the shiny polished black floor.

She was not ready to reclaim her shine…especially with a cute athlete who had fast girls throwing their Fruit of the Looms at him left and right. That was way too close to her mother's story. She wasn't ready for the foolishness of boys who grew up to be even more foolish men.

forty-one

Starr
October 6 @ 11:00 a.m. | Mood: Powerful

Starr still could not believe that her father's PR team had so quickly and efficiently spun the truth. She was still embarrassed, but at least now people were offering her condolences and not just snickering behind her back. Of course, now everyone was wondering what her mystery illness was, but at least they were too sympathetic to post pictures of her Fruit of the Looms all over the Net. Even her unknown nemesis, the Diva of Drama, gave her a pass.

She still couldn't believe that a simple kiss to the neck from Jordan had made her pass out. *What the...?*

"We still need to out who the Diva of Dumb is," Starr reminded both Dionne and herself.

Dionne shrugged. "She's the one sitting around watching us, talking about us and truly hating us because she can't be us. Haters are fuel. Gas me up. I don't care."

Starr laughed, wishing she had Dionne's spunk all the time.

She fingered her new diamond Rolex watch as they waited in the hall outside the cafeteria for Marisol. "She's on the way," Starr told Dionne, who was now applying a fresh gooey layer of lip gloss.

"You still haven't told us what all you got for your birthday," Dionne said as she capped the tube and dropped it back into her Gucci tote.

"And you never told me about the status of you and Reggie," Starr told her as a few students walked past them into the dining hall.

"You first."

She pointed to her watch and the pink Ricky bag on her arm. "And the kids at school got me a bunch of cute stuff like T-shirts with crazy sayings, makeup and stuff. Most of it we're donating to a couple children's hospitals and group homes. And of course the Gucci outfits and jewelry you and Marisol got me were purrfect."

Starr waited patiently as Dionne studied her nails. She cleared her throat.

"I'm not really feeling Reggie. But we'll see where it goes," Dionne admitted. "But he has stopped the pervert talk. Thank God. I had built a bridge and got way over *that* mess."

Starr laughed as she spotted Marisol through the window. "Marisol looks so cute today. Definitely four stars."

"Definitely," Dionne agreed, rising from where she was seated in a large windowsill.

"Things better with her parents?" Starr asked, genuinely concerned.

Dionne shrugged. "She doesn't talk about it."

The click-clack of Marisol's heels echoed down the length of the hall as she made her way to them. "Sorry I'm late, but I don't know how Beyoncé does heels all day, every day. Three inches are my limit."

"Fashion is pain," Starr told her, something out the window catching her eye. Jordan and Heather in the middle of a heated discussion. Lovers' spat? Whateva. Heather could have him because she was offering up something Starr couldn't compete with. *S-E-X*. Plain and simple.

"When are they going to pull Heather in the office for that crap she wears?" Starr asked, her eyebrows drawing together as Jordan turned to walk away, but Heather grabbed his arm.

"You talking about that extra-tight, coochie-cutting jumpsuit she got on?" Dionne asked as she turned toward the windowsill where she sat and looked out the window, as well.

Marisol joined them at the window. "I see London. I see France. I see Heather with no underpants."

Starr knew her friends were trying to help, but she kept her facial expression neutral…even though on the inside it really ticked her off to see them together. *What's that about?*

"Wonder what that's all about?" Dionne asked, taking the words out of her mouth.

They both looked on as Jordan snatched away from Heather and walked into the main hall. Heather dropped her head in her hands and it was obvious she was crying.

"Trouble in paradise?" Dionne speculated.

They watched as Heather suddenly bent over and threw up on the front lawn.

The Pacesetters let out a little gasp of surprise...and curiosity.

"Is she...preggers?" Dionne asked in a whisper that really wasn't a whisper at all.

"Oh. My. God." Starr felt like her mouth couldn't—wouldn't—close.

D-R-A-M-A! Times Ten.

"Oooooooh," Marisol said, like she was about to go run and tell. She clasped her hand over her own mouth.

They all stood there and watched as Heather ran toward the parking lot—and not the main hall, where the nurse's office was on the first floor.

At the scent of Gucci Rush cologne, Starr looked over her shoulder. Jordan stormed past them into the dining hall not even speaking to them, leaving the doors swaying back and forth in his wake.

The girls all looked at each other before they all spoke at once:

"Maybe it's the flu."

"Maybe she's just sick."

"Maybe she ate something bad."

Starr was the first to recover. That was the job of a leader. "Listen, we have more important things on our calendar than wondering about Jordan and Heather," she said, even though in her mind she was going to get to the bottom of it...and soon!

She plucked a piece of lint from Dionne's sleek ponytail.

She tapped her lips to suggest a fresh coat of gloss to Marisol.

"It's been a rough six weeks, girls. Plenty of people were waiting on us to fall, but we didn't. In fact, we're back bigger and better than ever," she told them. "Let's show them who runs this."

It seemed silly, but Starr wanted them to walk into the dining hall together now that her party had been a success—thanks to her planning and her parents' checkbook—and Marisol was back to fab status. Starr wanted all of Pace to know that the Pacesetters weren't going *anywhere*.

* * * * *

FROM THE AUTHOR

Hello, Everyone,

Thank you times a thousand for purchasing Pace Academy: *FABULOUS*. I hope you enjoyed the introduction to the Pacesetters clique and the rest of the students at the exclusive private school, Pace Academy, in Saddle River, New Jersey.

Yes, these kids have everything any teen could ever want or desire at their fingertips—designer clothes, high-tech gadgets, chauffeur-driven luxury cars, their parents' credit cards, wealth and fame. The spoons in their mouths are platinum and encrusted with diamonds. Even with the best things in life money can buy, there's still drama to be faced by all teens—whether they are rich or poor: rival cliques, gossip and rumors, jealousy, first loves and first heartbreaks.

Each of the Pacesetters faces her own issues with her desire to be/live/have the *Fabulous* life and in the second book in the Pace Academy series, the girls face the high price of fame. The drama continues…big-time. lol.

Stay tuned for more details and be sure to spread the word that the Pacesetters R here!

Best,

Simone

XOXO

ABOUT THE AUTHOR

Pace Academy: *FABULOUS* is Simone Bryant's first work of young-adult fiction. It is the first of a seven-book series about the Pacesetters clique. Simone Bryant is the pseudonym for Niobia Bryant, a national bestselling author of romance fiction, mainstream fiction and urban fiction.

For more on the Pacesetters series and its author, please visit:

Facebook: Simone Bryant—Teen Fiction Author
Twitter: www.twitter.com/beApacesetter
E-mail: beApacesetter@yahoo.com

Not every lesson is learned in school....

Second semester, second chances, and James "JD" Dawson has a lot to prove at the University of Atlanta—like shake academic probation. But JD once again finds himself in trouble—and what's worse, his future hangs on helping Kat get elected student body president. To do that, he'll have to learn who to trust and who's trying to play him—or his next ticket home will be one-way.

Coming
the first week
of January 2010
wherever
books are sold.

NEXT SEMESTER
Cecil R. Cross II

www.KimaniTRU.com
www.myspace.com/kimani_tru

KPCRCI450110TR

Are they rock-solid—or on the rocks?

Keysha's life is looking up! She has the lead in the school play and her boyfriend, Wesley, has moved back home. Perfect, right? Except that a backstabbing rival is scheming to get her role... and another girl is keeping Wesley busy while Keysha is rehearsing. With the prom on the horizon, the one relationship Keysha thought she could count on is looking shakier by the day....

Coming the first week of December 2009 wherever books are sold.

Decision Time
A KEYSHA Novel

ACCLAIMED AUTHOR
Earl Sewell

www.KimaniTRU.com
www.myspace.com/kimani_tru

KPES1721209TR

It's time to man up...

Avery has spent his entire life in Patterson Heights, a Baltimore neighborhood with a mean rep, but a good place to grow up. When a family tragedy changes Avery's life forever, he must prove himself all over again at a new school. He can't even confide in Natasha, the one person who seems to really *get* him. It's up to Avery to choose between doing what's expected and being true to himself....

Coming the first week of October 2009 wherever books are sold.

PATTERSON HEIGHTS
Felicia Pride

www.KimaniTRU.com
www.myspace.com/kimani_tru

KPFP1481009TR

Curveball, coming right up...

Indigo Summer and her best friend Jade are the best dancers on the high-school dance team. Now one of them is going to be team captain—Indigo just never expected it to be Jade. Jealousy suddenly rocks their friendship. And they're not the only ones dealing with major drama. Their friend Tameka is destined for a top college...until one lapse in judgment with her boyfriend changes everything.

Friendships, the team, their futures...this time it's all on the line.

Coming the first week of June 2009 wherever books are sold.

DEAL WITH IT
An INDIGO Novel

ESSENCE BESTSELLING AUTHOR
Monica McKayhan

www.KimaniTRU.com
www.myspace.com/kimani_tru

KPMM1410609TR

FRIENDSHIP.
LOVE.
FAMILY.
SCHOOL.
LIFE.
DRAMA.

IT'S ALL HERE.

www.myspace.com/kimani_tru

true to you™

www.KimaniTRU.com

KPTRUMYSAD09TR